AN UNDERGROUND SERIES PREQUEL

CHASING HEARTS

FROM USA TODAY BESTSELLING AUTHOR
ERIN BEDFORD

ALSO BY ERIN BEDFORD

The Underground Series
Chasing Rabbits
Chasing Cats
Chasing Princes
Chasing Shadows
Chasing Hearts
The Crimes of Alice

The Mary Wiles Chronicles
Marked by Hell
Bound by Hell
Deceived by Hell
Tempted by Hell

Starcrossed Dragons
Riding Lightning
Grinding Frost
Swallowing Fire
Pounding Earth

The Celestial War Chronicles
Song of Blood and Fire

The Crimson Fold
Until Midnight
Until Dawn
Until Sunset
Until Twilight

Curse of the Fairy Tales
Rapunzel Untamed
Rapunzel Unveiled

Her Angels
Heaven's Embrace
Heaven's A Beach
Heaven's Most Wanted

<u>**Academy of Witches**</u>
Witching On A Star
As You Witch
Witch You Were Here
Just Witch It
Summer Witchin'

<u>**House of Durand**</u>
Indebted to the Vampires
Wanted by the Vampires
Protected by the Vampires

Granting Her Wish
Vampire CEO

AN UNDERGROUND SERIES PREQUEL

CHASING HEARTS

FROM USA Today BESTSELLING AUTHOR

ERIN BEDFORD

CHILDREN IN THE FAE world are hard to come by. It's been twenty years since a child was born. Even longer since a royal child. So, it came as no surprise that when the Queen of the Seelie Court had a daughter, the whole Underground would come out to rejoice.

While the human world was celebrating their Yule, the residents of the Underground, the Seelie, and the UnSeelie Fae, came together in the grand hall of the Seelie Court. Higher and Lower Fae alike were welcome to party and pay respects to the new princess. For the first time in over a hundred years, no one was turned away from their doors.

The Queen and King of the Seelie Court stood at the front of the room upon a raised dais. They watched the crowd with matching blue eyes and both had hair as white as snow. They were fair and justice rulers and their people respected them above all else. Why else would they all come to see the newborn princess?

In middle of the dais, for the entire Underground to see, sat a cradle with gold and white ribbons and bows. Inside lay a tiny pink and wrinkled child, with hair as white as her parents and eyes as blue as the sea. Each citizen that passed by oh'd and awe'd at the little princess wrapped in a silken gown.

Her father, the king, placed a hand on the cradle and bent down to caress the top of his daughter's head. "You will be the light of the kingdom, my dear, just you wait."

"She won't be anything if we don't get this line moving," his queen responded back. Labor had been hard on her and the standing around was harder on her still. The king was surprised she hadn't blasted them all with how short her temper had been through her pregnancy. She had promised to try to keep her raging hormones in check; a snide remark was the least of his worries.

"Don't worry, dear, there aren't that many more." He pressed a kiss to the side of her head and wrapped his arms around her waist. "Besides, Seer hasn't even been through yet, and you so wanted to hear what he had to say."

Frowning, the queen patted his hand and nodded. "I suppose you are right, but next time we have a child we are making sure he is first in line."

"Next time?" the king smiled down at her with surprise. "You want more children?"

"Of course I do. It would be a pity for our little girl to grow up with no siblings to play with. Though, I do hope the next one does not kick as much." She made a pained face that made the king chuckle.

"We can have as many as you like, and we will proclaim that Seer is first in line for every one of them. That should make the old man happy."

The queen snorted. "If he is still a man at that point. You know how he is, changing his appearance every hundred years or so. Next time he could be a woman." Her lips curled up in the first real smile all evening. "Could you imagine? A female Seer. Now that is not something I would want to miss."

"Nor I." The king laughed along with her until his eyes caught sight of someone in the progression of visitors. "Now, here is someone you will be delighted to see I'm sure of it."

Coming up the dais in all of her dark glory was the UnSeelie Queen. Her dark hair was pulled back, and she wore a dress that shimmered in the light, she glided up the steps with her son, Dorian, at her side.

"Cousin," the queen held her hands out to her, "how wonderful of you to come. I haven't seen you since young Prince Dorian's last birthday." She pressed air kisses to each side of the UnSeelie Queen's cheek and then bent at the waist to greet the young prince.

"How are you, my dear?" she cocked her head to the side, taking in the child before her. In fae years he was already over fifty but in human years he still looked as if he had yet to reach his tenth birthday.

Though, the fierce intelligence that shot out of his eyes would never make anyone believe he was less.

"Fine," he growled between clenched teeth.

"Dorian!"

His sapphire eyes snapped to his mother, and he ducked his head at her chastising glare, his black hair hanging over his face.

"Sorry," he muttered, scuffing his foot on the floor.

"I'm sorry, cousin. He has hit that rebellious stage that demands he make everything a battle. I'm lucky to be able to get him out of the outskirts long enough to go to a lesson. He is obsessed with those damn opalaughts." She rolled her eyes at him. "You'd think as a fae, he hadn't seen a dozen or more in his lifetime. They do breed like rabbits." The dark haired queen shook her head, her hand placed on her son's shoulder to keep him from causing another outburst.

"No worries." The king chuckled; his eyes alight with glee. "I'm sure we will have our own hellion to worry about soon enough."

The UnSeelie Queen gave him a small smile in return before turning her gaze to her cousin. A frown marred her face as she asked, "I know it might not be the appropriate time, but while we are here, I was wondering if you had thought any more about that issue we had discussed before?" her voice lowered, and her eyes darted around to make sure she wasn't heard. "About the shadows?"

"No, I hadn't thought about it, and you are quite right, now is not the time to be discussing such depressing issues," the Seelie Queen snapped before letting a brilliant smile that did not reach her eyes cover her face, "It is a celebration after all. The humans can mark this day as Yule for the rest of time but today will always be the glorious day we had a Seelie Princess come into the world."

The king placed a hand on her waist, giving her a comforting squeeze. "Quite right. Quite right." He nodded his head, pretending not to notice the way his wife's magic flared against his hands.

The time to talk about what plagued their realm was fast approaching, but for now, the king and queen preferred to linger on happier thoughts. Their daughter would only have one time to shine and they wouldn't let it be spoiled by talk of shadows and such nasty things.

The UnSeelie Queen nodded in understanding though she wasn't content with their answer. She led her son down the dais and into the rest of the party all the same.

"She almost let it slip."

"But she didn't," the king countered, "your cousin is smarter than you think. She wouldn't want to cause an uproar in the kingdom anymore than you would. Have faith that she will do the right thing." He brushed his hand along the side of her face with a reassuring smile before his mouth widened as something behind her caught his attention.

"Ah, here he is now. See, I told you he would be along soon." The king opened his arms gesturing toward the next figure in the line.

"Yes, you did. Now go get him." She gave her husband a little push toward the one they had been waiting for.

The fae in question was an UnSeelie fae that was respected by all the

Underground. He wasn't royalty. He wasn't even pleasant. In most cases, he was a grouchy old fart who didn't care about anything but his pipe. One that he had, unfortunately, brought to the Seelie Princess's celebration.

"Seer, how nice to finally see you." The queen waved a hand in front of her face, trying not to sneeze at the sickly sweet smell coming from the pipe in his hand.

"Well, I would have been here sooner had you not invited the whole Underground." Seer sniffed taking a large puff from his pipe with one of his six sets of hands, his blue lips puckered around the end. His large belly filled most of the space between them as he adjusted his fuzzy coat, a darker blue than his own skin.

"I apologize, old man." The king clapped Seer on the back with a smile. "We couldn't hold back our joy. It had to be shared with everyone." He gestured a hand down to their daughter who had awoken from her nap to gaze upon the blue creature above her.

"I can see why you would." Seer took a step toward the cradle but was stopped by the queen who held her hand out to him. He looked down at her hand, frowning before handing his pipe over to her.

Seer leaned forward placing his top set of hands on the edge of the crib. His eyes, an obsidian color, gleamed under the lights as he called upon the magic that allowed him to see the future.

The king and queen watched in awe waiting for him to come out of his trance. The thing Seer was known for was just that, seeing things. The past, the present, and the future. All of them were open to him. Unfortunately, dictating what parts he saw was not.

Leaning back from the crib, he held his hand out to retrieve his pipe. Placing the tip of it in his mouth, his face creased in apprehension. Whatever he had seen was not something he wanted to share.

"Well?" the queen questioned, anxiety filling her at his silence.

He puffed out a cloud of smoke being sure to turn his head away from the child and then turned on his heel. He stopped at the bottom of the dais before changing his mind and coming back up the stairs.

"She will be beautiful and loved, like her mother." His words eased the tension in the king and queen's hearts. "But there is danger in her future and you must beware."

"Beware?" the king stepped forward clasping his hand with his wife's. "Of what?"

Seer became uncomfortable, shifting this way and that. He wouldn't meet them in the eye as he said, "Love."

"Love?" the queen cried out, her eyes dashing around her quickly before lowering her voice. "What do you mean? What does love have to do with it?"

"Your daughter will indeed be beautiful and loved by all that know her, but your love will be her downfall." His dark eyes locked with the queen's in warning. "Children are a great many things but hold on too tightly..." he shook his head as he trailed off.

"Thank you, Seer." The king ushered the man away, his eyes lingering on his silent queen.

Once Seer was well away, the king came back to his wife's side. She had a dazed look on her face as if she wasn't really there. Her hands were clasped in front of her, a confused frown etched on her face.

"Darling?" the king asked placing a hand on her shoulder. "Are you all right?"

Jerking away from his grasp, her eyes cleared, and she rounded on him with a snarl. "How could I be all right? He practically just said I was going to kill her with my love!"

"Shh!" he gestured with his hand for her to keep it down, the fae that were still coming through the line were starting to whisper amongst themselves about the queen's display.

"Calm yourself, my love." He grabbed her by the shoulders and looked her in the eyes. "Remember, Seer only sees what might happen in the future, not what will happen. And what he says isn't always what he actually saw. You know this. Don't take what he said to heart, we will love and care for our daughter as if he has said nothing at all."

"But that's what will hurt her, don't you see?" she pushed his hands away and went to the edge of the crib. Her eyes gazed down at her little baby girl. Her heart ached in her chest as she watched her smile at one of the brownies that had been making faces at her.

How could she ever hurt such a precious thing? From the moment she was born she had been her world. The very thought that she could hurt her in any way was foreign to her.

"I won't let anyone ever hurt you. My daughter, my precious Lynne." The queen held her daughter in her arms, all the love she had pouring down on the little princess. But inside, inside her heart had begun to freeze and ice.

GROW. I THOUGHT AS I pressed my magic into the dirt surrounding my fingers.

My magic swirled inside my stomach and then shot up and out through my fingertips. Bright green strings of light spread through the earth, filling it with life. I smiled as sprouts popped up all along the dirt bed in the royal garden. I pushed just a bit more magic into the ground before leaning back on my heels.

Dusting the excess dirt off of my hands, I surveyed my work. Many would think being able to give life to plants was a small thing but I say they can stuff it.

Plants were one of the best gifts the world could give us. All plants needed was water, sunshine, and love. They didn't argue. They didn't try to manipulate you into doing things you wouldn't normally want to do. Unlike Fae, particularly, my mother.

"I knew I would find you here," my father's voice, a deep timber forced me from my thoughts.

"Where else would I be? It's not like I'm allowed to leave the palace." I didn't even try to hide the bitterness in my voice.

"Now, daughter, don't be like that," he started, kneeling down beside me but I jumped to my feet, the dirt that had gathered on my skirt fluttering to the ground.

"I have a name," I snapped.

My father, Oberon, King of the Seelie Court, may look like my brother to an outsider with his flawless skin and shiny pale-colored hair, but he was actually closer to a century than my measly hundred. The only feature that gave away his age was his eyes. Wise and weary from all his years, even they could not hide all he had seen. I only wished he would trust me enough to tell me.

"You know the rules, daughter." He stood to his feet, an understanding look on his face. "We are not to use our true names anymore."

"It's a stupid rule. Even mother does not abide by it."

"Your mother lives by a different set of rules than we do." He shook his head. "But the rule is in place for a reason." When I opened my mouth to argue he added, "One that cannot be argued. Even if you do not understand it."

Crossing my arms over my chest, I turned away from him. I wasn't going to get anywhere with him.

The Fae world was all about rules. You can't do this, you can only do that. But more recently, and the most annoying was the new one about saying your real name.

It was utterly ridiculous. No one was going to get taken because the shadows whispered at him or her in the dark. At least that's what they said would happen.

Call me a skeptic but I didn't believe it.

"Anyway, I am here on a more important matter than arguing about what cannot be changed," my father continued.

I frowned. I knew what he wanted to talk about, and I didn't want to talk about it anymore than he wanted to fight about mother and her stupid rules.

"Now, I know that it's not how you imagined you would find your spouse but it really is for the good of everyone." He placed his hand on my shoulder and spun me back around to face him.

"You mean good for Mother," I spat.

The soothing look on my father's face changed to that of concern. "Your mother just wants the best for you as do I. And we both agreed this would be the best way to keep you safe."

"And gain more power," I snorted, "Don't try to pretend like this is about me. It's all about Mother not being settled with enough. She will always want more power and she will give up anything to get it. Even her own daughter."

My father sighed and dropped his hands from my shoulders. "I don't know why I even bother. You are headstrong just like your mother."

"Only good bit I got from her," I muttered.

That wasn't exactly true. My mother, Queen Titania of the Seelie Court, was known to be the most beautiful of the realm. With long pale blonde hair and ice blue eyes, she was the envy of everyone at court. Sadly, I had taken after her looks, and by my father's judgment, her temperament.

Too bad I couldn't force myself to not feel anything like she did. If I could kill one of my own kind as easily as she did, then I probably wouldn't care about who I married, only about when I would get my next fix.

Though, killing a Fae wasn't as easy as just lopping their head off. No, my mother was crueler than that. She'd rather throw them to the Shadow Realm to waste away on their own rather than do the dirty deed herself.

When she wasn't out casting half the kingdom, the rest were imprisoned in glass mirrors. Which to me was a fate worse than death.

I glanced down at the plant that was thriving from my magical touch. It was bad enough I was forced to stay in the palace. If I were locked away from the light and air it would kill me, no need to wait for my powers to wane.

Moving my gaze from the plant and back to my father I asked, "When is this so called betrothed showing up, anyway?"

"The UnSeelie Prince will be here within the fortnight. You should prepare to look your best for the occasion. We want to make a good impression." My father's lips ticked up slightly, obviously relieved that I wasn't going to argue anymore.

My face scrunched at his words.

I'd never been out of the palace, so it was no surprise that I didn't know anything about the UnSeelie Court aside from what I read about in books.

While they had some of the most beautiful High Fae, it was said that their Lower Fae were not more than animals. The Seelie Court was all about structure and playing the game of Court. The UnSeelie Court preferred to wear their emotions on their sleeve doing whatever they liked whenever they liked with no thought to the consequences around them.

Tucked away in the library they had seemed so fascinating to me, and now I would not only get to meet one but I was to marry one. I couldn't imagine how that would go. Would they throw me over their shoulder like a barbarian and drag me back to their kingdom? Or would they not even wait until the wedding night and ravish me on the ballroom floor?

The thought of either caused a flutter of excitement and terror to fill me. Thankfully, my father's voice pulled me out of my panic.

"Daughter?"

My eyes jerked to his, and I nodded. "I will be fine. Don't worry."

No UnSeelie Prince would make a fool of me. I'd make sure of it.

CHAPTER 2

DORIAN

THE GLASS SHATTERED AGAINST the wall. The piercing scream from the irate woman in my room made my ears ring.

"I can't believe you are doing this to me!" a luscious brunette snarled at me, her state of undress not a worry to her.

My eyes briefly drifted down to her bared breasts before I sighed and rolled my eyes. "I am hardly doing anything to you. It is not like I have a choice in the matter."

This didn't seem to placate her any, because she stomped her foot and growled, "You are the crown prince of the UnSeelie Court, you don't answer to anyone! If you didn't want to get married, then you wouldn't have to do it."

I ran a hand through my own dark hair, the length of it brushing the middle of my back. It should probably get cut soon. I didn't want to displease my bride to be. But who knew what kind of men she was into. If she were anything like her mother than it didn't matter what I looked like, she'd hate me either way.

"Are you even listening to me?"

I sighed once more. I really didn't need this now. "Of course I am, Bianca." Stepping over to her, I slid my arms around her waist drawing her soft form against my hard chest. "Let us not fight. We do not have much time left before I am to be exiled to the other side." I tried to kiss her, but she turned her head away from me, her ruby red eyes glaring at me.

"Oh, no, you don't." She placed her hands on my chest and shoved me away. Marching over to where her discarded clothing lay on my bedroom floor, she jerked them on. "I am not just some toy you can take out of your drawer and play with whenever you like. I have feelings, Dorian."

"Could have fooled me," I muttered.

Bianca and I had only been seeing each other for a few weeks. I thought we had both been on the same page. My reputation didn't exactly paint me as the flowers and romance kind. I'd rather explore the hills and valleys of the female body than explore the depths of our feelings. For Reaper's sake, I didn't even know her last name or favorite color. It was hardly a basis for a relationship. Her outrage was completely uncalled for.

Not bothering to put my own clothing on, I crossed my arms over my chest and waited for Storm Bianca to subside. Unfortunately for me that didn't look like it would happen anytime soon.

"And another thing! If your mother thinks that marrying off her only son to that ice queen's brat will help our kingdom, she is crazier than Hatter!"

The mention of the silver-haired Seelie Fae that currently resided in the dark forest made me frown. I didn't know his story exactly. He'd come to my mother seeking refuge from the Seelie Queen's rage a few years ago. My mother, of course, had granted it, as I would have done as well. Everyone was welcome in the UnSeelie Court. We weren't biased to looks and power like other Fae. But there was something about the man that was unsettling. Something had happened to him on the other side but he would never say what, no matter how much I asked.

Shrugging off the thought of the Hatter, I grabbed my trousers from the floor. "I trust my mother and so should you." I dragged the pants on while giving Bianca a pointed look.

"Of course I trust the queen." Bianca's expression quickly softened. She placed her hand on my chest, her eyes down as she stroked my chest. "I just don't like it."

Placing my hand on hers, I gave it a tight squeeze. "I do not care for it either but we deal the cards we are dealt. And it is my turn to play the game."

Her lips turned down in a frown. "Be careful. Those Seelie aren't like us. They wear their smiles like a suit of armor. You won't know if they will strike until it's too late."

I chucked her under the chin and smiled. "Do not worry about me, dear Bianca. I play to win and I never lose."

I sent Bianca on her way with the promise to call for her when I came back from meeting my new bride. Then with the heavyweight of duty on my shoulders, I made my way to the orchard.

The UnSeelie Court was a precarious mistress, ever changing on a whim. It made the best defense against outsiders, but it was a headache for anyone who wished to map the land. It had never bothered me. I loved the land more than any woman I had ever been with. I enjoyed rediscovering her curves each day. I would certainly never bore of her like I would have other women.

My feet sank into the soil as I stepped into the orchard, the only place that never changed and my haven from the rest of the Fae world. Rows and rows of trees filled the area. There were workers that cared for the vegetation, I was sure of it, but I had never seen them. Lower Fae like those who worked the fields were more of the shy type. They preferred to do their work away from prying eyes. Not that I could blame them. I would not want to be gaped at all day either.

Sighing, I leaned against my favorite tree that sat above all the others. I could see the whole orchard from here and they had the most delicious oranges, far superior to any other I had ever tasted. Here I could relax and let my troubles roll off me.

I took a deep breath in and let it out slowly. Then frowned. The heaviness was still there. It usually worked but for some reason today my haven wasn't doing it.

The brush of fabric against the ground pulled my attention from the view. I didn't need to turn to see who it was. Only one person would dare bother me here.

"Hello, Mother."

"Hello, darling." Skirts as black as night came into view. As a child, the gowns she wore always reminded me of spider webs. When I had told her she had just laughed and patted my head. "Dorian dear, you are more perceptive than you know."

I hadn't known then what she meant, but now I knew that she wrapped herself in clothing such as that to put up a defense. While the Seelie Court might hide behind their smiles, my mother hid behind a fearsome facade. One that most of her citizens knew was just a mask. No, Mab was softer than mush but had a wicked temper if betrayed. I'd only witnessed it once and the thought of it still made my spine tingle.

"What are you doing out here?" She stood by my side not touching me but her presence was comfortable, nonetheless.

"Thinking."

Her dark blue eyes, so much like my own crinkled at the corners, her lip ticked up at my answer. "You mean, procrastinating."

I shot her a smile. "That as well."

Her head fell back as she laughed, the smooth surface of her face contorted showing her age. If anyone didn't know us, they would think we were siblings. The rate at which we aged made it almost impossible to tell who was the parent and who was the child. It made for interesting situations at parties that was for sure.

"Ignoring the obvious reasons you are hiding," she cleared her throat with a hand over her mouth, "while you are leaving another has come."

"Oh, really?" I asked my brow quirking up.

"Yes," her eyes sparkled, "a small little thing with golden curls and a peculiar disposition. Could make for some interesting events to come."

Shaking my head at her, I laughed. "Your interest in the humans is so strange. They are pests that are better left to their own devices. Having them in our world is not good for any of us. Say one of them goes missing?" I asked my lips pressed into a line. "Then they would be beating down the door of our world in moments. Don't think for one moment they are our friends."

She placed her hand on my arm; the blood red of her nails glinted dangerously. "You worry too much. We need them as well, you know. They depend on them to survive. One here and there won't hurt anything. And besides," the smile on her face was positively wicked, "she's just a child. How much trouble could she cause?"

I didn't have an answer, but I had a sinking feeling in my gut telling me that this child could cause more trouble than any of us could ever imagine.

CHAPTER

3

LYNNE

RIDICULOUS! THIS WHOLE SITUATION was utterly and completely barbaric. My shoes made angry sounds as I stomped through the hallways of the palace. I'd just come from my mother, where she had requested my presence with the Court.

She never requested my presence. If she had her way I'd be locked away in a tower only brought out for special occasions. I sometimes wondered why she even bothered to have me at all.

Any other time I'd have been overjoyed to go to court but this time I'd have rather stuck my head in the dirt. Not only did she want to talk about my upcoming marriage, but also she had to ask in front of everyone if I was prepared to do my wifely duties. She might as well have asked if I was ready to spread my legs for a complete stranger rather than being coy about it. The whole court had laughed at my blushing face either way.

If she wanted me to be prepared, she shouldn't have kept me so cooped up all these years. The only experience I had with men and sex were from books and the stories my best friend Erydesa told me.

Unlike me, she could do what she liked and when she liked, which she took full advantage of by sleeping her way through most of the royal court. Fae weren't prudes by any means, but to someone like me that wasn't even allowed to be alone with a male, it seemed a bit extreme.

Even when she retold the tales of her nightly and sometimes even daily activities, I couldn't help but be in awe of her and the whole aspect of sex. Some of the things she has had done to her or have done to others made me laugh and blush. Who used feathers as a way to get in the mood? And being tied down? I couldn't imagine ever giving up that much control to someone else.

The thought of what my future husband might like crept up, but I quickly shook it off. I didn't care what he liked. I wasn't marrying him. I'd sooner die.

My face settled into a firm determination as I made my feet start toward the library. Rounding a corner I bumped into a hard chest and almost lost my footing. Large hands grabbed me before I hit the ground and a familiar chuckle filled my ears.

"Pardon me, your highness." Bastian, Erydesa's twin brother, grinned at me. His hair was almost as white as my own, but his blue eyes were more of a muddy blue. He and Erydesa had the same position on sex and dressed to show off their assets. Having grown up with Bastian, the first time he started going without a shirt my face had heated to volcanic levels. Then when he had pierced his nipples I couldn't look at him for days.

My eyes went to the glinting jewels on his chest and my face heated. I forced my eyes to look to the side causing Bastian to laugh. Miffed at being laughed at I pulled away from him and smoothed my dress down. "What are you doing here Ba—

Jewels," I caught myself before I called him by his real name. These nicknames were really irritating though I didn't need to ask why Bastian had decided to go by Jewels.

Not mentioning my slip up, Bastian moved back into my personal space. "I wanted to check on you of course."

"Why?"

"Well, you know, after what happened in court I thought you might need a shoulder to cry on." He picked up a piece of my hair and twirled it between his fingers. I had the sudden urge to wash it again. It was no secret that Bastian wanted me. He'd come on to me enough times I would think he'd take the hint that I wasn't interested. Unfortunately, he was one of the few males my mother let me be around. If all the other males were like him I wasn't sure I wanted get to know them.

"I'm all right," my lips twisted, and I slowly withdrew from his touch and added, "But thanks for your concern."

I moved around him and resumed my path to the library where I hoped to drown myself in some ancient literature. Bastian, on the other hand, couldn't take the hint, as usual. I rolled my eyes as his footsteps echoed mine.

"Did you need something else?" I asked, my eyes forward hoping if I was dismissive enough he'd leave me be.

We came up on one of my favorite hiding spots and without a word, Bastian grabbed my hand and pulled me into the darkened corner.

Struggling against his hands, confusion filled my face. "What the hell?"

Bastian's hand straddled either side of my shoulders as he leered at me. "Come on, your highness. Let's not pretend any longer."

"Pretend what?" I raised a brow at him.

"That there isn't some kind of attraction between us." One of his hands came up to stroke the side of my face and I flinched away from him. "Your mother has a point."

"What?" Anger overwhelmed my disgust. My mother was never right.

"You need to be prepared. You aren't like my sister and I. You are delicate. Innocent." He plucked at the collar of my dress, and I shoved his hand away. Bastian sighed and dropped his hands.

"I'm just trying to say that we are counting on you to make this alliance work, and that means you need to keep that UnSeelie bastard happy."

"Keep him happy?" I exclaimed. "What about keeping me happy?" But it was like I wasn't even speaking.

Bastian grabbed me by the hips and pressed himself against me. "That's where I can help you."

"Help me do what exactly?"

"Help you learn how to please him, of course." Bastian ground against me, letting me feel the hardness between his thighs. "Don't you want your first time to be special? For the one who takes you to be someone you know? Not with some stranger who doesn't give a shit about you other than to gain power?"

Having had enough I conjured up some of my magic and shoved at him, forcing him off me. Bastian's eyes widened, and he lost his balance causing him to crash to the floor. My lips formed a tight smile as I stared down at him.

"Now let me help you, Jewels," I scowled, "I am High Fae, and while I might be inexperienced in some areas of the world, I am also the daughter of one the most powerful Fae in the whole Underground. No one will be taking me." I turned away from him but then paused and glanced over at him still sprawled out on the ground. "And for the record, it would never be you. Never."

The sound of Bastian's cursing was music to my ears as I stomped away. Help me? I snorted. If anyone needed help, it'd be that UnSeelie Prince. He didn't know what he was getting into, and if I had my way, he'd be the one eating out of the palm of my hand. Not the other way around.

CHAPTER

4

DORIAN

WE ARRIVED EARLY IN the morning. And when I say we, I mean two guards and me. The Seelie Queen wouldn't allow me to bring any more people. More than likely she didn't want any more dirty UnSeelie crowding her palace.

I snorted, causing one of the Lower Fae unpacking my things to look up. The short, meek male could have been High Fae had they been taller and more attractive. I honestly was surprised the Seelie Queen would lower herself to let anyone not like her even be in the palace, let alone handle anyone's things. But for all, I knew the Lower Fae could have been assigned to me because I wasn't worthy of one of her own serving me.

"Your highness?" the servant asked, his eyes down.

"Nothing." I shook my head and then paused. "Wait, what can you tell me about the princess?"

At the mention of the princess, the servant's eyes darted up from the floor and then quickly back to the ground. "The princess is wonderful. A warm embrace in a cold winter storm." The love and adoration in the servant's voice surprised me even more so since he kept going. "There are no words to describe her beauty and grace. The very definition of—"

"I get it," I cut him off, "she's a goddess."

"No! Not a goddess," the servant cried out but then quickly lowered his voice. "A goddess would not seek to acknowledge those lower than her. Her Highness is beyond any of those such things. You are a lucky Fae indeed to be engaged to such as she."

"I see," I drew out raising a brow at him. I wasn't sure how I felt about marrying someone who was thought so highly of by her people. It was great for being a leader, not so much when trying to woo them.

"Is there anything else I can help you with, your highness?"

"No, no. That is all. Thank you." I waved him off and turned back to the room they had put me in. Thankfully, the servant hurried out of the room and I was alone once more. The room was furnished well enough, but it was nothing compared to the room I had back home and it wasn't going to help me with the princess.

Scrubbing a hand over my face, I sighed. I had only just gotten here, and I was already ready to go home. Fortunately, I'd only had a few encounters with Seelie Fae throughout my last hundred years or so. The few times I had gotten together with them hadn't been pleasant. Everything took effort. Every word, every facial expression was being judged all the time. One wrong look at the wrong person and you could find yourself in the Seelie Queen's dungeon. I'd heard it was even worse than being exiled to the Shadow Realm, and I could believe it. Speaking of good impressions, I doubted the queen would like it if I wandered her halls in mud covered clothing.

I dragged my shirt off letting it fall to the floor. I thought for a moment to just leave it there, let them think the man they were giving their precious princess to was a slob but remembering the servant who had coward, not daring to meet my gaze made guilt eat at me. Sighing, I leaned down to pick up the shirt from the ground. Throwing it onto the bed on my way to the wardrobe, I dug through my clothes and frowned. I really shouldn't have let my mother pack for me. There was nothing but frills and furs. Sometimes I wondered if she had wished for a daughter.

Rolling my eyes, I grabbed the shirt with the least bit of frills and paired it with a pair of black pants. There was one thing my mother, and I had in common and that was our love of black. There wasn't a speck of color in my wardrobe, which was just the way I liked it. Compared to the Seelie I would stick out like a sore thumb.

The thought made me smile. It would piss the queen off to no end for sure. A knock on the door drew my attention away from the wardrobe. Before I could answer the door, it was pushed open and a long legged blonde walked in.

"So you're him, huh?" the unimpressed sneer on her face did nothing to mar her beauty. Long pale hair swung behind her as she strutted into my room. The high slit in the dress she wore gave me a glimpse of her shapely legs when she took a step. The sparkle in her eye when I finally met her gaze told me she knew I was looking, and she knew how good she looked. No way this was the princess.

"And you are?" I gestured to her as she stopped in front of me. Her eyes roamed over me, pausing at my bare chest that I couldn't help but puff out at the attention.

"Don't worry about me. It's you who you should be worried." She pointed a perfectly shaped nail at me.

"Is that so?" I smirked and crossed my arms over my chest, which drew her attention to my biceps. She gave them a long appreciative look before sniffing.

"You listen here, princey."

Princey? I laughed to myself but didn't respond.

"The woman you are going to be marrying isn't just some slop that you can use once and toss aside." I opened my mouth to defend myself but she cut me off, "Don't think we don't know about your reputation. Women talk, even across realms." the positively lethal tone of her voice made me flinch.

"She's worth way more than her mother is trying to sell her off for." The bitterness that had come into her voice caught my interest. So far everyone loved the princess but hated the mother. It was good information to tuck away for later.

"I am beginning to see that," I responded, catching her off guard. Slipping one arm and then the other into my shirt I let it hang off of me without buttoning it up. "Your princess seems to have quite the fan base."

My visitor opened her mouth, but I kept going, "But since you have heard of me. I am sure you are aware of my tendency to win, and while your princess might be fantastic and all, that does not make her immune to my charms."

This made the woman laugh, but I ignored her and continued, "My mother wishes me to marry the Seelie Princess, so that is what I will do and no one, not even the princess herself will keep me from getting what I want. Do you understand?" I tipped her chin up with a smug grin.

The blonde seemed dumbfounded for a moment before she busted out laughing. Pushing my hand away, she shook her head. "You keep thinking that, princey." She laughed once more and headed toward the door. Stopping at the doorway, she glanced back at me one more time before chuckling again. "This is going to be fun." She snickered before closing the door behind her.

Well, that wasn't encouraging.

I SAT IN THE library with my legs thrown over the side of a chair. I was so immersed in my book that I didn't realize anyone had come in until a pair of hands covered my eyes.

A wide grin spread across my face as I giggled. "Gab!"

"How did you know it was me?" my best friend, Erydesa, also known as Gab, dropped her hands.

Shaking my head, I dropped my legs and closed my book. "Because you are the only one immature enough to do such a thing."

Ignoring my comment, she grabbed me by the arm and dragged me out of my seat. "Come on. I know you've been in here longer than is healthy. You need to get some fresh air."

I snorted but let her lead me out of the library and down the hallway and out into the gardens. I had no doubt that she had something up her sleeve. Erydesa rarely did anything for anyone's good but her own.

"Did you hear? The UnSeelie Prince arrived today." She wasted no time saying as she walked arm and arm with me along a path in the garden.

"I had heard such news." More than one person had told me today that the UnSeelie Prince had arrived. Some were delighted to let me know, others more in a cautionary tone. Of course, most of those came from the servants. The High Fae wouldn't be caught dead showing me their worry.

In fact, the very servant that was assigned to attend to his royal pain in the butt, Gerald, had come to me just before Erydesa had. The quiet Fae had explained everything that had happened with the prince. Including, how he had asked about me. What Gerald had told the prince about me was flattering and not at all true, but I could just imagine what the prince must think of me now. The thought actually made me smile.

Gab chuckled beside me. "Don't sound so excited about it. Someone will start to think you care about your betrothed."

"Hardly." I snorted, playing with the ends of my pale blonde hair. "Everyone knows that this is a marriage of convenience. Nothing more."

"Sure it is, but have you seen him yet? Don't you want to know what he looks like?" Smiling at me, Gab trailed a hand along the metal fence lining the garden path.

I quirked a brow at my friend's mischievous grin. "Why would I want to do that? I'm supposed to marry him whether or not I approve of his appearance."

"Well, I would want to know whose bed I'll be warming for the rest of eternity." Gab stopped in her tracks, pulling me with her. "And as you are my best friend and confidant, I did a little reconnaissance on your behalf."

"Of course you did." I rolled my eyes. The younger Fae always needed to know what was going on with everyone in the palace. It was for her own pleasure and hardly a selfless act in the name of friendship.

Gab sniffed. "Well, if you're going to be like that, I don't think I'm going to tell you what I found out." She stuck her nose in the air, pretending to be cross.

"Yes, you will. You can't help yourself." I dropped her arm and continued down the path, my attention half on the surrounding flowers.

Having never left the palace, I'd seen them all hundreds of times over. I'd never even seen all of the Seelie Court, but I was supposed to marry a complete stranger, and live with him all for the sake of solidifying our defenses against some shadow creature?

The hope of leaving the palace was the only reason I even considered the sham of a marriage, to begin with. If it gave me the chance to be free, to see new places, and to finally walk through the halls of my own home without the fear of who would lose their heads next. I didn't need to know what my husband looked like. I'd marry him all the same. Though, I'd be damned if I made it easy for him.

"Oh all right, you've talked me into it." Gab gave an exaggerated sigh and hurried to catch up with me. "You know all you had to do was ask."

"But I didn't ask."

Gab ignored me and continued babbling, "So, I went down to the guest wing where they keep all the important people. Not that UnSeelie royalty is all that important, but anyway, I got stopped by one of his brute guards–"

As she told her story, I could feel the excitement as it radiated off her in waves. She always got this way when she had some juicy tidbit that she wanted to share. It was nearly impossible for her to keep a secret.

"–And then I said, I have as much right to be here as anyone." She scoffed. "Can you believe that? He actually thought I was a servant! Me! The thought of me cleaning." She shuddered.

"Maybe he didn't know." I shrugged my shoulders, pretending to show interest in her distress.

"Ha! Do I look like a lower Fae? No. Look at these cheekbones." She gestured toward her face. "Fae have killed to be as pretty as me."

I rolled my eyes. "Gab, that was one time, and they didn't die. They only ended up scarred."

"She might as well have died. I would have committed suicide if I had to go the rest of my life disfigured like that." Gab made a face at the thought.

"Not everyone cares about appearances." I offered and then tried to change the subject. "I thought you were going to tell me what he looks like, not his guard."

"I'm getting there." She waved me off. "So, I got past the nasty guard and into the prince's sitting room, and low and behold there he was lounging on the couch like some half-breed. Really now, does he have no decorum? It is no surprise he wouldn't think twice about letting his guard down where anyone could walk in on him."

"He was in his private rooms, though. No one should have been able to walk in on him," I pointed out, not really believing much of what she said. Erydesa had a way of adding on to her stories to make them seem more than they were.

"But I did, so anyone else could have as well. I'm just saying, he should be a little more mindful of where he is, even if he is a guest. He is still UnSeelie. He could have–" Gab stopped mid-sentence catching sight of something in the garden. "Oh pooh, I was just getting to the good part."

I followed her gaze to land on a dark-haired Fae sitting on a bench with a book in his hand. With his attention focused on his book, my eyes trailed down his exquisite form. All thoughts of not caring about looks were smothered by a sudden undeniable need. When he glanced up from his book, my breath caught in my throat.

Eyes the color of the glittering night sky locked onto mine. The fierceness in his gaze froze me in place. There was anger there, but also a hollowed emptiness. I knew at that moment I'd go through with the engagement. Not because I craved freedom or because he made my insides melt, but to make sure those beautiful eyes never gazed at me with such loneliness again.

DORIAN

AS FAR AS GARDENS went, the Seelie garden was above average. Nothing compared to the virtual Garden of Eden my mother had at home, but it was nice nonetheless.

Finding my way there had been a challenge though. It was like I was a pariah. No one wanted anything to do with an UnSeelie, even a royal one. I hadn't felt so unwelcome since I'd walked in on a faerie mating ritual. I shuddered at the memory. Now that was something I never wanted to see again.

When I had finally found it I'd been about to get one of the servants to direct me to the garden, as I'd already been wandering the palace for a good while.

I found the first bench I could and splayed out on it for a bit. I had just started reading my book when the sound of voices filled the area. As they got closer, there was one that I recognized.

The female from earlier.

My brows furrowed and my face hardened. I didn't take kindly to being laughed at and even more so that she was now talking to her companion like I was a piece of garbage she had stepped on. UnSeelie or not, I was still the crown prince; she needed to show the correct respect to her superiors.

I was all set to put her in her place when they rounded the corner, and I froze. While she had pale hair like the other woman, her blue eyes held an icy stare. This was without a doubt the Seelie Princess. She resonated royalty and was the spitting image of her mother. I realized then why the woman had been laughing at me so much.

This princess was no pushover.

"Why hello again." The woman from before smiled as they approached, there was a hint of amusement in her eyes that irritated me to no end.

"Hello." I snapped my book shut and stood to my feet. "I don't believe I got your name before."

"Ah," the blonde seemed to flush before clearing her throat and placing a hand on her chest, "I am Gab."

I couldn't help the smile that spread across my face. Her name was absolutely ridiculous. Of course, it was probably not her real name. The new rule about keeping your birth name secret had spread across the realms, not that everyone had actually followed them. I was bad about it myself.

Clearing my throat, I gave a slight bow. "It is a pleasure to meet your acquaintance, Gab." Straightening back up, I turned my gaze to the other blonde still clutching her companion's arm. "And you must be my beautiful betrothed. I have heard so many glorious tales about you that I feel as if I know you already."

I held my hand out to her, waiting for her to place her hand in mine. After a moment or so, it was obvious that she would not be allowing me to kiss her hand as was customary. In fact, she was gazing at me in such an odd manner I feared she might be dumb. Was it possible that everyone loved her so much because of some disability?

No. There was no way the Seelie Queen would allow herself to have a disabled child. A Fae so set on perfection, the very thought of it probably horrified her.

Thankfully, Gab seemed to think that she was behaving oddly as well. The blonde tried to discretely nudge her princess causing her to jolt out of whatever daze she was in.

"Oh, uh, sorry," the princess stumbled over her words, her face coloring a delightful pink. I fought against the need to grin at her. If it was this easy to get her to blush, I couldn't wait to see how she would react when I started to woo her. The thought made parts of me harden. My arousal was not unnoticed by the two Fae women. The princess's face heated even more, but Gab had a smug sort of smile on her face.

Sometimes I wished our senses weren't so advanced. It was impossible to get away with anything without our scent changing.

I'd have to remember in the future to refrain from thinking naughty thoughts that might give me away.

"And obviously, I am delighted to meet you as well." Pretending not to have given away my position was pointless, so I might as well use it to my advantage. The princess must have a better hold on her hormones, or maybe I just didn't affect her the same way she affected me.

Nah.

Gab giggled and even when her princess gave her a sharp look she kept laughing. "Are all UnSeelie as overeager as you?"

The accusation was so offensive I didn't know how to respond. Of course, we weren't. I was just losing my mind.

"Not that I am aware of. So, can you speak or am I to assume you just don't want to speak to me?" I tried to turn the subject away from my arousal and back to my mute betrothed.

A slight smile spread across her mouth and my eyes were instantly drawn to her full lips that just begged to be nibbled on and would look fantastic wrapped around a certain appendage.

"I don't know about her but I find your conversation invigorating." Gab's laughter filled her voice, but I ignored her, my eyes solely on my betrothed.

Her pale eyes flickered down and then back up as she chewed on her bottom lip and then she spoke, "Believe me, the pleasure is mine."

The words were so quiet that I almost didn't hear them but the voice was clear. Like bells, it tinkled a rhythmic sound that caused my body to tighten even harder. This made Gab laugh even more.

Damn. What was wrong with me? I don't remember ever being this out of control of my body even when I was an adolescent. Maybe it was the innocent way she blushed at my gaze or the slight quirk of her lips at her friend's laughter but I had a bad feeling this was going to be harder for me than I thought.

CHAPTER

7

LYNNE

"THE PLEASURE IS ALL mine? Really?" I smacked my hand against my face while Erydesa laughed at me from my bed. Glaring, I pointed a finger at her. "And you weren't any help at all."

Swallowing her laugh, Erydesa held her hands out to each side. "What? It's not like I knew you'd freeze up worse than a troll on mating day."

I rolled my eyes as she burst out laughing again while tossing around on my bed.

"I did not freeze up."

"Did too! You said not one intelligent word the entire time we were with his royal deliciousness." Erydesa's eyes glazed over and she licked her lips. I didn't need to smell the air to know she was attracted to my betrothed. Not that I blamed her. He was quite something to look at.

It wasn't like I hadn't seen my fair share of attractive men. The Seelie Court was littered with them. My mother wouldn't have it any other way. Beauty was everything to the Seelie Queen. Even the Lower Fae she used as servants had to be a certain level of attractiveness. I didn't know when she became so shallow or power hungry. I felt like she'd always been that way. Though, my father would argue that.

"I don't know what happened," I mumbled staring out the window. The sky was beginning to darken, which meant my first dinner with my betrothed was quickly approaching. Thankfully, I wouldn't be alone, but it was a mixed blessing. My parents would be there and that came with a whole other set of problems.

"Well, you better get a hold of yourself quick," Erydesa said sliding off my bed and approaching me. "I've heard about this guy, and he's a smooth talker. He'll have you on your back before you even realize you are being seduced. Though," her eyes twinkled with a wicked gleam, "with how he reacted to your presence alone, I don't think you will have a problem guessing what's on his mind."

We both giggled.

No, I definitely wouldn't have a problem telling what my Fae prince was thinking. I had only heard rumors about the UnSeelie, but it seemed like the talk was true. The UnSeelie didn't control their emotions the same way the Seelie did. Which put me at an advantage in a major way.

"So," Erydesa started, "what are you going to wear to this dinner?" she brushed past me and opened my wardrobe where she thumbed through my clothing and frowned. "Don't you have anything more... just more?"

"Unlike you," I pushed in beside her and grabbed one of my better dresses to drape over my arm, "I don't spend all my time in the company of the opposite sex. So forgive me if my wardrobe is lacking a certain provocative luster."

Erydesa eyed the pale colored garment in my hand with a disappointed look.

"Come, now, your betrothed has given you the perfect weapon against him and you aren't going to take advantage of it?" She pulled the dress out of my hands and held it up. "At least wear something with a bit of cleavage. This just screams virgin."

Jerking the dress from her hands, I snapped, "I am a virgin."

She shrugged. "So, doesn't mean you need to look it."

"He didn't have a problem with what I was wearing before, so why change?"

"To drive him wild of course."

I shook my head at her, not even bothering to argue. We would always have differing opinions on how we should portray ourselves, and there was no use wasting my breath on it. My everyday clothing had easily aroused the prince; purposely showing more skin would be showing my hand. I'd rather keep my moves subtle. So I could keep him on his toes until I had him right where I wanted him. One thing I knew for sure about this arrangement, I would be the one with the power, no one else. I was done being pushed around.

METAL CLINKING AGAINST PLATES was the only sound to accompany the awkward silence that filled the dining hall.

Normally I dined alone in the library or with the servants. My parents were usually too busy entertaining to eat a meal with me. I couldn't even remember the last time we sat down together to eat, so sitting with them now made the situation even tenser than it should have been.

I felt bad for the UnSeelie Prince. He wasn't used to the intensity of my parents. My eyes watched as he shifted in his seat, his eyes darting around him like he was waiting for someone to jump out at him and attack at any moment. It took all my effort not to smirk at his discomfort.

"So," my mother finally broke the silence. Her sharp gaze locked onto the prince not missing a detail. "What do you go by?"

"Excuse me?" the dark haired prince's brow rose and genuine confusion filled his face.

"Well, we can't very well call you your highness now can we?" My mother glanced at my father and me and gave a dirty chuckle. "You must have some kind of name to which we can refer to you by?"

My betrothed's face actually reddened at my mother's question. "No, I suppose not." His eyes met mine, and I gave him a reassuring smile but quickly dropped it.

You're supposed to be making this harder for him not easier, I chastised myself. I couldn't seem to help myself when it came to this man. There was something about him that just made me want to save him. Whether from my mother or from himself I wasn't sure.

"Most of my citizen's call me the dark prince. I suppose you can call me that as well." As soon as he said his name, I had to hold back my laugh. I didn't do a good enough job though because a strangled noise came out causing the dark prince's eyes to snap to me. I covered up my slip up by taking a drink from my glass.

"And what about my bride to be?"

His words caught me off guard causing my drink to go down the wrong pipe. Coughing, my eyes watered as I croaked, "What?"

"What do you wish me to call you?" His dark sapphire eyes glittered with laughter. "Or would you prefer just wife?"

Before I could answer my mother burst out laughing. "I had forgotten how amusing your kind are. I will have to remember to invite more of you to my gatherings. Don't you think, dear?" She clasped hands with my father who had a tinge of a smile on his face as well, but the strain around his eyes told me he wasn't as happy to be here either.

"Whatever you say, my love." He gave my mother a tight smile, but his eyes never wavered from the UnSeelie Prince.

For all my father's convincing to get me to agree to this marriage, now that it was actually happening and right in front of him, he didn't seem too thrilled about it. Or trusting of my betrothed. Was it just fatherly concern or something more?

Unfortunately, I was unable to answer that question yet because everyone's gaze turned to me, waiting for me to answer the question. "I... I don't know." I frowned hard. I'd never had to think about a nickname. As the princess, everyone just called me your highness anyways or my parents called me daughter. Unlike Erydesa, I didn't have an outstanding trait like talking too much or body jewelry like Bastian. It was in that moment that I realized how utterly boring I was.

"Then shall we name you now?" my betrothed suggested causing all of our eyes to turn to him.

"I think that's a splendid idea." My mother clapped her hands together with a gleeful smile. "Since you are soon to be taking my daughter as your own, I think it is only fitting you do the honor. Don't you think, daughter?"

My jaw clenched at being referred to as if I were a piece of property. I smiled tightly. "Of course, mother."

The dark prince didn't say anything for a moment. His eyes roamed over me taking in every inch. I felt a slight twinge in parts I had never felt before at the intensity of his gaze. It caused the dark prince's nostrils to flare and his eyes to turn stormy. Shifting in my seat, I didn't dare meet my parent's eyes. They no doubt could tell that my scent had changed, and that was too horrifying to even contemplate.

Finally, when I felt as if I could no longer bare his stare, he spoke, "Peach." The single word caused a liquefying effect on my insides. Not the word itself but the way he said it. Dark, forbidden. As if he were talking about more than just a name. It caressed my flesh and coaxed my magic, asking me to let it in. And Reaper help me I really wanted to.

CHAPTER 8

DORIAN

SITTING IN MY GUEST room, I ran over the events of the evening. I didn't know why I chose that name for my future wife. She wasn't a piece of fruit. But all I could think of was her creamy skin and the way she smelled. Sweet and juicy, I couldn't wait to take a bite out of my blushing bride. Waiting to take her until she was ready would be torture but well worth the wait.

I had no doubt in my mind that my future bride was untouched. She blushed far too easily.

Then there was her reaction to the name I gave her. I didn't mean to put so much magic into the name. It had just happened. The effect it had on her though was worth it.

If I thought she smelled fantastic before, the way she smelt after my magic touched her made a primal force ignite inside me. Never with any of my prior lovers had I been so taken by another. It had taken all I had not to jump across the table and take her right there in front of her parents.

I snorted. Knowing how the Seelie were about sex, I wondered if they would have even cared. Their parties were known to get quite physical. The guests becoming so drunk on faerie wine that it was not unheard of for an orgy or two to sprout up in the midst of the ballroom.

Thinking of those kinds of parties made me frown. How was my peach so untouched with the world she lived in? The fact that she had not taken a lover or two over her lifetime was suspicious.

Not that I was complaining. I didn't want to have to compete with any past or current lovers. Not to forget the thought of being her first and only lover made the alpha in me roar with delight.

I adjusted the painful tightness that had been constantly plaguing me since the moment I saw my peach. If I didn't get some relief, I would have a full night of tossing and turning. The morning could not come faster. I wanted to see her again, but this time without her parents or annoying friend by her side.

If only I could get her alone, then I could put her fears at ease. I was sure she had many. Fae weren't very trusting. And asking a Seelie Fae to trust an UnSeelie was like telling the sun to stop moving across the sky. Thinking of seeing her again caused my magic to jerk. It didn't want to wait either.

And why should I? She was my betrothed. We were practically married anyway. Why shouldn't I visit her now?

Standing from the couch, my feet moved toward the door. Once out in the hallway, I froze. I had no idea where her bedroom was or if she would even be in there.

Placing my hands on my hips, I took a deep breath in trying to find some hint of her sweet scent. I caught a faint whiff. It was old, not something I could really follow. More than likely it was from weeks ago. I doubted she frequented the guest's quarters often.

Since I couldn't rely on my sense of smell, I would have to use my magic to guide me. I twirled my hand in the air and blue light filled my palm. Not too bright to draw attention to me but bright enough that I could keep an eye on it without losing it. I pushed my intentions into the ball of magic, urging it to find the one we both wanted to see. It didn't need much convincing, it was more than happy to seek out our bride to be.

The blue ball shot down the hallway, and I quickly followed after it. It took me through many turns and down a pair of stairs. No one stopped me or even paid any mind to the hovering ball guiding me. The Fae I did see only gave me a brief curious glance before continuing on their way. I guess I wasn't that interesting. Other times, I would be bothered by my anonymity but in this case, it was a blessing.

One more turn and the ball stopped at a large double door room. I stood before it waiting. Was this it? It had to be, my magic was never wrong.

Absorbing the ball of light back into myself, I poised my hand before the door and let it pound against the wood. My ears strained to hear some kind of response, but I couldn't hear anything from inside the room. My brows furrowed, and I leaned slightly toward the door.

"Can I help you?"

Jerking back from the door, my eyes landed on the very person I had been searching for. Wearing a much different outfit than I had seen her in at dinner, she still took my breath away. While the majority of the women seemed to be partial to wearing gowns that clung to their figures there were a few who wore trousers and tunics. But none of those who I have seen wear such clothing compared to seeing it on my betrothed

The legs of the pants hugged her hips and outlined her shapely legs making my mouth water. Her neck and shoulders were bare in a long-sleeved cream-colored shirt that tied just above her bust. Suddenly, my mind was thinking of all the ways I could get her to let me untie those ties.

"Hello?" her brow raised, and she waved a hand in front of my face. "Are you just going to stare all day?"

Licking my lips, I cleared my throat. Pulling something flowery out of the air, I tried to make up for my stumble. "If the vision was you, then I could gaze upon your beauty until the Reaper takes me."

Her lips pursed together, and I could see my words did not have the desired effect. If anything, it made her even more suspicious of my showing up on her doorstep.

"What are you doing here?" she crossed her arms over her chest and pushed one hip to the side. The sight didn't help my desire to touch her.

Sighing, I decided to go for the truth. "I apologize if I startled you. I did not mean to make you uncomfortable." I ran a hand through my hair and gave her a sheepish look. "I simply thought it might be nice for us to get to know each other without Fae politics getting in the way."

My peach watched me for a moment and then nodded. Moving toward me she slipped between the door and myself. She swung the door open and gestured inside. "After you, dark prince."

Her lips quirked as she said the nickname which gave me hope. It was possible this wouldn't be so bad after all.

CHAPTER 9

LYNNE

SAYING THAT I WAS having a mild panic attack was an understatement. I'd never had a male in my room that wasn't a servant or a relative. Why I had let a complete stranger in without a thought was beyond me.

"So, this is your room," the dark prince drew out as he stepped into my room. His head turned this way and that.

Becoming self-conscious, I searched the room for any clothing or embarrassing items that I needed to hide. Luckily, though, I am a pretty neat person, and the only things lying around were my books.

I made a mental note to take some of them back to the library before I stepped in front of my betrothed. "So what did you want to talk about?" I might as well get the ball rolling before he did something to make me lose control again like at dinner. The thought of it still made my face heat.

His dark eyes turned from looking over my room to meet mine. His lips turned up in a small smile and he shrugged. "Anything. We do not have anyone to worry about now that we are alone. So feel free to be yourself."

Be myself? In front of a complete stranger? That was as likely to happen as a faerie giving birth to a troll.

Clasping my hands together in front of me, I tried to think of something safe to talk about. But my mind was blank. I honestly had no idea what to talk about with this person.

"How about this, let us have a seat and each take a turn asking a question?" he asked sitting on the couch in the middle of the room. He patted the seat next to him, clearly wanting me to join him, but I hesitated.

Closer was probably not a good idea when it came to the UnSeelie Prince that already made faeries dance in my stomach.

He leveled his gaze at me and smirked. "Come, now, I won't bite. I'll be a perfect gentleman."

I chewed on my lip glancing at where he sat and then looked away before sighing. At least it wasn't on the bed.

I eased down next to him, my hands in my lap. The dark prince shifted in his seat and I tensed for an attack. When all he did was cross one leg over the other, guilt ate at me.

Come on, Lynne, pull it together. You can't just jump to conclusions like that. You aren't your mother.

"So," the dark prince started, placing an arm on the back of the couch. My body was acutely aware of how close his hand was to my shoulder.

"So," I replied feeling a bit foolish.

"What do you like to do for fun?"

I couldn't help but laugh a bit at his question. When he gave me a curious look, I gestured around us. "You can't tell?"

The dark prince's eyes landed on the pile of books I had next to us, and he smiled sheepishly. "I suppose that one was pretty obvious."

"You think so?" I teased.

"All right then." He turned slightly in his seat to face me. "Since I wasted mine, it is your turn."

"All right," I paused, my eyes staring off into the distance and then I had my question. My pale blue eyes locked with his. "Do you really want to marry me?"

His eyes widened a fraction. I seemed to have stunned him. Maybe I shouldn't have asked? No. I needed to know. If I was going to make the effort, then he would too. I refused to be miserable for the rest of my existence.

After what felt like forever, he finally answered, "You do not waste any time, do you?"

I shrugged a shoulder. "Best to get the hard ones out of the way. So, do you?"

"I am going to be honest with you, my peach." His nickname for me caused my skin to prickle. I forced the feeling back to listen. "When I first learned of our engagement I did not react well."

I could relate to that. Seven plants died at my hands because I was so furious and couldn't control my magic. It had taken weeks before I could finally get it together well enough to coax a sprout from the ground.

"And now?" I asked partly holding my breath for his answer.

"Once I realized it was for the good of our realms, I could not exactly say no." He offered me a small smile.

"I get that."

"Once I was set on it, I could only hope that you were not some spoiled brat that I couldn't stand. Thankfully, that was no so."

My lips quirked up at that. "You didn't care if I was ugly? Or deformed? What if I had horrible breath? Or my laugh was annoying?"

He laughed at my questions, the sound of it made me shiver. Was there nothing about this man that didn't affect me? If I reacted this way just to his laugh, I couldn't imagine how I would react to his touch.

"It did cross my mind, but then I thought, the Seelie Queen would not dare to have an ugly child. So I should be safe, and thankfully, I was right." His eyes glittered as he watched me. "My turn."

"All right," I answered, though, he hadn't exactly answered my question at all.

The dark prince leaned forward his eyes darkening as he said, "Have you ever laid with another?"

The question stunned me. I had expected all sorts of questions. I hadn't expected him to ask something so personal. Though, I should have. We are to be married, eventually. He should know whether I have been with another. Though, based on what Erydesa had said about his reputation, I had no doubt that he had been with plenty of women.

"No." The single word seemed to resound through the room making him suck in a hard breath.

"Have you ever even been kissed?" he asked getting closer to me.

"That's two questions," I whispered, my eyes flickering to his lips and then back up to his eyes where they had turned into the turbulent stormy blue.

"I do not think that you have." His hand came up to brush the side of my face, his voice lowering as well.

My body burned where his hand was touching me, and the room suddenly was stifling. I leaned into his touch without meaning to; my eyes fluttering opened and closed.

The dark prince's thumb slid along my bottom lip, and my tongue darted out, tasting him. It was then that my nose was assaulted with the combination of our scent. It had kind of earthy spice to it. Something I had never experienced before.

But having experienced it now, my body roared in response. My body alighted with desire and a low growl came from my betrothed, causing my eyes to shoot open.

His nostrils flared, his eyes even darker than before. It was as if he were a feral creature and not the Crown Prince of the UnSeelie Court. The intensity of his gaze frightened me enough that I tried to pull away, but his other arm wrapped around me drawing me closer to him until our fronts touched.

"I wish to kiss you."

The words were more of a statement than a question. I wasn't sure how to react. I wanted to kiss him too, but part of me kept telling me not to. That he would ruin me if I gave into him. I shoved that part back and swallowed thickly before nodding.

That was all the consent he needed before his mouth covered mine. He didn't take his time coaxing me into submission. Instead, he dove in overtaking my senses until all I knew was him.

Each sweep of his touch ignited a fire in me that left me craving more. My hands grasped his shirt, hoping for something to ground myself, but all it did was spur him on more. I was hopelessly lost in him and I couldn't have been happier.

CHAPTER

DORIAN

EXCITEMENT STIRRED IN MY belly as I walked my mother's garden. Today was the day. My peach would finally come to my home and meet my mother.

I had been exiled to the Seelie Court for over a month, and while I had made progress with my betrothed, she had yet to let me kiss her again. Just thinking about it made my blood stir with desire, and I longed to have her by my side.

I hoped that being in the UnSeelie Court helped her relax a bit. Just like her mother, she was wound so tightly that I worried she would burst from all the words she didn't say and the feelings she barely suppresses behind her pale eyes.

It pains me to think of her cooped up in her palace. She is like a wildflower that should be free to spread her roots among the masses, not kept down in the dark.

I chuckled to myself. Who would have thought I, a notorious womanizer, would be spouting poetry like some lovesick fool?

But was I a fool? My peach had so easily claimed my heart, I didn't even know it was happening until I had caught myself smiling just watching her care for her plants. Or even when I would catch her in the library. So engulfed by her reading that no one else in the world mattered. Even the way her face scrunched down in concentration made me hard. Reaper help me, but I was hopeless.

"I hope you are not worrying yourself too much?" my mother's voice jerked me from my thoughts and I turned to greet her.

I wrapped my arms around her small frame, pressing my lips to her cheek. "Oh, you know me." I gave a small smile before releasing her.

"Yes, I do. Is this child really all you claim to be?" Her eyes narrowed into a warning look that I knew too well. I hadn't been a very well behaved child.

"Do not worry, mother." I placed a hand on her cheek and hoped my expression was reassuring. "You will love her as much as I do. And she is hardly a child. She is almost as old as me."

"You are not more than a toddler yourself." My mother sniffed before turning her gaze to her garden.

The pride and joy of the UnSeelie Court was my mother's flower wonderland. Rows of flowers of all shapes and colors lined the courtyard. A large fountain sat in the middle of a large tree with a man and two women. I had asked about the fountain before but my mother had just smiled that secret smile of hers without ever giving me a real answer. My eyes moved from the fountain to a bush near us.

"They haven't budded yet," my mother mused, "they probably won't be ready until you are wed."

"That's all right," I replied walking over to the bush, "It can be a wedding gift then."

As soon as I got home from the Seelie Court, I had asked my mother to help me plant a rose bush. White roses for my bride to be. I wanted her to feel welcome in what would soon be our home, and I thought that if she had a plant that was just her own it would help her transition without feeling like an intruder.

"Not that I'm complaining," my mother started making me roll my eyes, "But why is it that she is moving here and not the other way around?"

I actually didn't know the answer to that one. When I had asked my peach about it, she had pursed her lips and said, "That is how my mother wants it."

It made me dislike the Seelie Queen even more. If she cared so little for her daughter's wellbeing, I could only imagine how much she cared for her own people.

Before I could come up with an answer for my mother, a crash sounded in the distance followed by a high-pitched scream. A horde of opalaughts came charging through the garden.

Mother and I jumped to the side so as not to get run over by the small rabbit-like creatures, matching frowns marred our faces. One opalaught brought up the rear of the group. It was smaller than the rest with ears so long they trailed behind it. When it came upon us, its eyes widened. So interested in my mother and I that it tripped over one of its ears, causing it to fall face first onto the ground.

Reaching down, I scooped the creature up in my arms. It wasn't very heavy, not much more than a few pounds, but its fur was the softest thing I had ever felt. Its body shook in my hands, obviously terrified.

"Do not worry, little one," I murmured rubbing a finger between its ears. "I will not hurt you."

It stared up at me for a few more moments before seeming to decide I was safe enough. It pushed its face into my hand trying to get me to pet it more.

Once I was sure I had its trust, I asked, "Can you tell me, little one, what has caused you to run?"

"Trip runs because of the mean girl, Trip does," his tiny voice explained, his beady eyes looking toward where he had come from.

"What mean girl?" my mother asked stepping closer to me.

The creature called Trip glanced to my mother, his mouth spreading out to smile. Everyone seemed to love my mother and why wouldn't they? She was far better than the other option.

"The human," Trip whispered as if it was a big secret.

My mother made a disgusted noise in the back of her throat. "I told you that child was going to be nothing but a pain. I better go see what she has done now."

She pushed by me toward where the opalaughts had fled from, her skirts brushing angrily against the stone path. I patted the creature on the head and sat him on the ground.

"Off you go. Let us take care of this."

Trip's little cotton tail wiggled behind him. "Of course, of course! Trip will leave it to your Highnesses, he will!"

What a peculiar little creature. I shook my head as it scampered off. I then turned on my heel to follow after my mother who had disappeared behind one of the many large green hedges.

"You must be more careful," my mother's voice rang out as I came into range.

"But I can't help it. They're so cute!" a bell-like voice replied.

Coming around the next corner, my eyes landed on the human girl the opalaughts had been so frightened of. She was a tiny thing dressed in a robin egg blue tea dress. She wore little white gloves on her hands and stockings on her legs. Her curly blonde hair bounced around her as she enthusiastically spoke to my mother.

"Hello, I do not believe we have met." I approached them with caution in my step. The child lifted her head. When her eyes landed on me they widened a fraction and then she was up on her feet and barreling into me.

Startled by the sudden contact, I placed a hand on top of the curly head to keep us both from going down. Her large eyes peered up at me with an innocent grin.

"I am the UnSeelie Prince, and who might you be?"

If possible, her grin expanded even further across her face as she clung to me tighter. "I'm Alice. Alice Liddell."

CHAPTER

11

LYNNE

SEVEN MONTHS. IT HAD been seven months since I had met and fell helplessly in love with my dark prince. My lips slid up into a smile at the thought of the UnSeelie Prince being mine. Giggling, I skipped down the path and out into my soon to be mother-in-law's garden.

After our initial meeting, it had been decided by both parties that it would be best if I spent some time in the UnSeelie Court as well. I, of course, had been delighted to finally get out from under my mother's thumb. But the UnSeelie Court was nothing like the palace back home.

For one, the air seemed sweeter. I didn't know why but each breath I took left a sweet taste on my tongue. It was peculiar for sure but not the only difference.

The moment I had crossed from the Seelie Court to the UnSeelie it was as if a weight had lifted off of me. I was suddenly not worried about how I acted or who saw me. I could smile and laugh without worrying what Fae might be plotting against me.

For once in my life, I felt truly free. I just hoped it would last.

"Wow," I murmured to myself as my eyes took in the surrounding garden. I thought mine was something to behold, but this place was like a wonderland of flowers. There were some here that I didn't even know existed.

My slippers padded against the cobblestone as I made my way around the enclosed area. The heavy scent of the foliage filled my lungs to the brim. There was no place I'd rather be than surrounded by greenery. Well, maybe my library, but the queen's garden was a close second.

"Do you like it?"

I jumped in place at the voice. I spun on my heel to meet the gaze of the most beautiful Fae I had ever seen. Everyone said my mother was beautiful, and that I was the spitting image of her. Not that I would take that as a compliment most days, but the woman before me now redefined everything I knew about beauty.

Her black hair was so dark blue streaks glinted in the light. It fell over her shoulders and blended into her matching dress causing a waterfall of silk. My hand itched to touch it. Was it as smooth as it looked? I forced my hand to stay put. This was my soon to be mother-in-law it wouldn't do to act out of place at the beginning.

My dark prince's eyes were the same as his mother's. Though his made my stomach twist in delightful knots, hers were full of mirth and a slight darkness that warned me to tread carefully. This was not a woman to trifle with.

"It's lovely," I finally answered back, my eyes turning from her to gaze around the garden once more. "I didn't know you had an affinity for the earth."

"Among other things." The queen gave a slight chuckle and moved toward me, her long form-fitting dress sliding around the stone. While most would have looked out of place in such grand attire she seemed to fit the scene perfectly. And of course, she would it was her garden.

She stopped beside me and my body tensed. I was used to my mother. I'd only met the UnSeelie Queen once before and I'd been a baby at that time. Now I didn't know how to act or speak. Did I call her your highness? Or Queen? This whole no name nonsense made things increasingly more complicated than it needed to be.

"I was looking for my betrothed," I explained, not wanting her to think I was snooping around. "Have you seen him?"

"He's in the orchard," she replied and then to my surprise she looped her arm through mine and began to lead me down the path.

"Where are we going?" I let her guide me toward an opening in the large green hedges surrounding the garden.

"You want to find my son, do you not?"

"Yes, but I just assumed you'd tell me how to get there." I took in every twist and turn we took in case I had to get back on my own.

She gave my arm a slight squeeze and smiled at me. "What kind of mother-in-law would I be to let you wander alone in a strange place? Besides..." her voice dropped an octave. "The UnSeelie Court is much more dangerous than it seems. I would not care to see you hurt from negligence."

I nodded not knowing what to say to her warning. So far the UnSeelie Court was much nicer than my own. Though, I hadn't been outside the palace walls, so my opinion was pretty much null and void.

We turned a few more times before we exited the hedge maze and stepped into a large field full of rows and rows of trees. My mouth dropped open at the sight. I'd never seen anything like it. The more I was in the UnSeelie Court the more at wonder I became.

"My son should be just over that ridge over there." The queen pointed her finger to the right where there was a slight hill and even more trees.

When she let go of my arm to leave I called out, "Wait? You're leaving? I thought you didn't want me wandering alone?"

She paused and gave me a slight smile. "Do not worry, there is nothing here that can harm you. It's one of the few places you do not have to fear but remember," her eyes narrowed, "there is much to fear in this world and your heart. Do not let either catch you off guard."

Chewing on my lip, apprehension filled my chest. Her words were not comforting. If anything, it made me even more anxious for her to stay. But before I could express my concerns she had reentered the hedge maze leaving me utterly alone.

My eyes searched the area expecting something to jump out at me at any moment. Even though she had said I was safe here, I still didn't like being left alone in a strange place.

After a moment or so, I took a deep breath and forced my feet forward. Staying here wasn't going to solve anything. I had come to find my dark prince, and that was exactly what I would do.

It didn't take long to make my way across the orchard and to the hill the queen had pointed out. When I got to the top of the hill, I found myself slightly out of breath and my dress sticking to my skin. It was a lot steeper than it looked.

At the top of the hill was a tree, much larger than the others with giant balls of fruit decorating its branches. My gaze didn't stay on the tree for long because below its branches stood my prince talking to a blonde woman.

Her hand touched his arm and a broad smile spread across her face as she laughed at something he said. Jealousy flared inside me as I approached the two. When I was within a few feet, the blonde's eyes caught sight of me. Whatever she had been saying was cut off causing my prince to turn.

"My peach," his sultry voice greeted me and he moved from the woman to my side. His arms embraced me filling me with warmth, and for a brief moment I forgot about the unknown woman and just enjoyed his closeness.

"Hello." I held him tight. "I couldn't find you at the palace. Your mother brought me here."

"Of course she would." He pulled back from the hug and brushed my hair behind my ear. "I am happy you arrived safely. I meant to be there when you arrived but something came up."

"Something?" My eyes glanced back to the blonde woman that had yet to be introduced.

The dark prince gestured to the woman to come closer and everything inside me screamed for her to stay away. But I held my tongue. I didn't know this woman or her relationship with my betrothed; I couldn't hate her just because of my jealousy.

"This is Ms. Liddell. She is visiting from the human world."

The blonde dipped down in a curtsy, her eyes sparkling with mischief.

"It's a pleasure to meet the one who has captured our dark prince's heart."

I didn't understand the laughter that filled her voice.

"That's enough out of you." My prince scowled at her and waved an arm. "The Hatter is no doubt waiting for you."

Ms. Liddell's lip puffed out in a pout and she stomped her foot slightly. "Fine, but don't blame me when you mess it all up." She flounced away in the direction I'd come from, leaving me completely bewildered.

"What was that all about?"

His hand came to rest on my shoulders and he smiled. "Do not worry your lovely head about her. Humans are even worse than faeries at times. Always putting their nose in where it does not belong. Now," his arm curled around me drawing me to his side, "let me show you my kingdom."

As my prince prattled on about the orchard and whatnot something ate at me. I couldn't put my finger on it exactly. I just knew that something about that woman did not sit right. I didn't just have the UnSeelie Court to fear but her as well.

CHAPTER

DORIAN

I THOUGHT OVER ALL that had happened in the last few months as I waited by my favorite tree in the orchard.

It was like a dream that I never wanted to end. My peach was everything I never knew I wanted and more. Sweet and caring but also with a lightning temper that when turned on me only served to make me want her more.

I had been firmly against the marriage arrangement when my mother had first told me about it. Even as I told myself it was for the good of the kingdom, I expected to end up in a loveless marriage with someone I couldn't stand to be around.

Now, I couldn't imagine being with anyone else.

I had spent the majority of my time with my peach and had been severely lax in my duties. I knew we would have to come out of our own little bubble eventually, but I needed more time with her before I returned to overseeing the UnSeelie Court with my mother.

My eyes glanced up to the sky where it had begun to darken. I turned around searching for my blonde goddess's head but didn't see it. She should be here by now.

Since it wasn't exactly appropriate for us to spend alone time in either one of our bedrooms we had taken to meeting up at my favorite spot. Each night, after dinner, I would wait for her to meet me. Usually, it was just before the last light shone.

But tonight she was late.

Growling in frustration, I started down the hill determined to figure out where she was when her voice called out. I paused mid-step and turned my eyes toward the voice.

My peach came running out of the entrance to the hedge maze, out of breath, and slightly worn for wear. A worried frown marred my face.

"Are you all right?" I asked when she stopped before me. Her hair was mussed and her clothing covered in a thin layer of dirt. Even a mess she was still the most beautiful woman I had ever laid my eyes on.

"I apologize for being late, but I got lost." She thumbed back toward the entrance. "Your mother wasn't kidding when she said the maze had a mind of its own. I thought I was turning the right corner but then the next thing I knew I was in this graveyard like place."

Oh no. I knew where she had ended up and it was no place for someone of stature to be.

"You didn't happen to run into any small creatures about this big." I held my fingers up about three inches apart.

"Yes!" She pointed at my hand. "They kept yelling at me in a language I didn't understand and then they attacked for no reason whatsoever!"

I sighed. "That would be the Veil of the Faeries. A bunch of pains in my side is what they are. They don't really need a reason to attack. If you come into their territory, you are free game."

"Then why don't you get rid of them?"

"They have their purpose as do many of the unpleasant creatures in the UnSeelie Court. Now, let us talk of something else more pleasant. I only get you for a short while before they will miss you." I wrapped an arm around her shoulder and led her to the tree.

I didn't want to worry my princess by telling her what the faeries were really used for. No need to make her panic, or with her curious nature make her want to examine them further.

Keepers of the deceased Fae, the faerie were temperamental and territorial. The only Fae they didn't attack were my mother, myself, and the Reaper. I wasn't sure he was actually a Fae. I'd only encountered him a few times, and each time was unpleasant at best. As I'd told my princess, each of us had our part, and we played them the best we could.

"So, how was your day?" she asked as we sat down beneath the tree and leaned against the base of the trunk.

"You were with me for most of it," I smirked at her.

Giggling, she smacked me on the arm. "That's beside the point."

"Well," I pretended to think for a moment, "There was this gorgeous princess that I have been dying to get alone all day. I think I might be in love with her."

"Oh really?" She quirked a brow at me. "Is she prettier than me?"

"Oh most definitely." I turned in my seat placing my hand on her hips.

"That's not very nice." She laughed and pushed at my chest. "You are supposed to say no one is prettier than me."

I cupped the side of her face and lowered my face to hers. "No one makes my heart race like you do. No one makes my blood boil with desire like you. There is no one in this world or the next that will have a hold on my heart like you do."

"Now that's more like it," she murmured before I captured her lips with mine.

Sliding my hands into her hair, I moved until I was hovering above her. I didn't want to move things too fast. Unlike myself, she has not had lovers before and I don't want to scare her away.

But my peach once more surprised me. She spread her legs beneath me and grabbed my hips, drawing me between them. The press of my center against hers caused me to groan. Encouraged by her movements, I cupped her breast in my palm kneading it gently. Moaning at my touch, she arched her back pressing more of herself into my hand.

As our tongues moved along each other, I pushed the length of her skirt up her legs, loving the smooth expansion of the skin beneath my hand. Moving up her leg, I sought out her warmth but frowned when her hand caught mine.

"Wait."

I pulled back to see her face clearly. "Am I moving too fast?"

"No, no," she quickly said, placing her hands on my hips to keep me from moving away. "I want you and I don't want to wait any longer but first…"

She trailed off chewing her bottom lip. Her eyes searched around us as if she expected someone to be watching. But I knew that no one would dare intrude on us. Not if they knew what was good for them.

"What is it?" I asked. "You can tell me anything, you know that."

"It's silly, really." She gave me a small smile that clenched at my heart.

"If it bothers you, I highly doubt it could ever be silly." I stroked the side of her face with the back of my hand.

"It's just...we are about to do something I've never done before and I..." she paused and held my gaze for a moment, "I don't even know your name."

I couldn't stop the smile that crept up my face. My silly peach.

"Is this you asking me?"

Her eyes narrowed at my teasing. "Not if you are going to make fun." She started to pull away from my grasp, but I grabbed her around the waist and flipped us over so that she was on my lap.

"I do not mean to make fun of you." I held her close to me. "I find the new rule ridiculous and if it had been any other time, we would have already settled this matter."

"Then why can't we settle it now? No one is around to listen in on us. It would just be between us two."

I stroked my thumb along her pouting bottom lip. Lovely. She was so breathtakingly beautiful I didn't understand how I had gotten so lucky. The fates must have decided to bless me with this gift and I wasn't about to waste it.

"Dorian."

Her head jerked up at my words and the smile that spread across her face lit her face like a beacon. She leaned in close to me, her lips barely brushing mine and whispered, "My name is Lynne."

CHAPTER

13

LYNNE

THE UNSEELIE QUEEN HAD been right. Her court was far different from my own. And even more dangerous.

When I first arrived, Dorian had wanted to show me his realm but was very hesitant to show me anything that might scare me away. Everywhere he had taken me was tame.

A flower garden that sang. A nest of opalaughts that were the cutest creatures I had ever laid eyes on. Mainly places that were in the direct vicinity of the palace.

But today was different. Today he was going to take me out of the palace area and into the heart of the UnSeelie Court. My excitement kept me up almost all night and had me up before the first light hit my bedroom.

"You are in a good mood this morning." Dorian smiled at me as we walked through the gardens.

"I'm with the man I love and about to go on an adventure, how could I not be anything other than happy?" My face hurt from how much I was smiling.

"I could think of something that would make you even happier." Dorian's hand slipped into mine and I curled my fingers around his, holding him tight. Ever since the first time we made love, we had not been able to stop touching each other, a caress here, and a stolen moment in the hallway there. I could live forever in his embrace and die a happy princess.

"Oh no you don't," I giggled and bumped shoulders with him, "You aren't going to distract me today. Today we are going out into your realm. I want to see everything. No more trying to shelter me." My lips curved down in a frown. "I got enough of that from my mother."

Dorian stopped and pulled me to him. "I am sorry. I do not mean to coddle you." He stroked the side of my face and I leaned into his touch. "I just know how dangerous my realm can be, and I do not want you to get hurt."

"When we marry I'll have to rule this realm too," I grabbed his hand in mine, "how can I be a good ruler if I don't know the people?"

"Very well," Dorian sighed and then smiled, "if you insist upon learning about the people then I will take you to see the craziest creatures that I know. That will keep your expectations low for the future."

Laughing, I let him drag me out of the garden and into the UnSeelie World. This would be an interesting day indeed.

WHEN WE STEPPED OUT of the queen's garden, I expected to end up back in the graveyard with the nasty faeries, but instead, we were at the edge of a forest.

"Wow, you weren't joking when you said your world changes a lot." My eyes took in the surroundings.

The tall walls of the hedge maze were at our backs and to the front of us were dark trees with rolling mist along the ground. I couldn't see much more than a foot into the dense forest and it gave me an unsettling feeling.

"This is why you should not wander on your own until she is used to you."

My eyes snapped to Dorian. "She? The UnSeelie Court is a woman?"

Dorian's lips curved up, his eyes twinkling. "Not in the physical sense of the word. But we refer to her as such because of her temperamental moods. One day she might be kind enough to let you get to where you wish to go and other days she'll move your house right out from under your nose. Quite irritating actually." His eyes narrowed at the tree line as if it were the very being he was talking about.

"Hmm, I could see how it would be difficult for someone new to your world."

"But it is an excellent defense mechanism." Dorian winked at me before taking my hand. "In any case, we better get going or we will be late for tea."

"Tea?" I asked as I let Dorian lead me over the forest line and into the dense fog.

The sounds coming from the forest were not like anything I had ever heard before. I would have imagined there would be animal noises and maybe leaves brushing against the branches of the trees but each step I took further into its depth the more it felt like I was in a moving breathing being.

"Yes," Dorian answered unaffected by the world around us. Did he not feel the brush of the wind against him, the way it pulled at you almost trying to keep you in place? Or maybe it was just me? Was it the UnSeelie Court trying to warn me away?

I sent a silent message to the mercurial being that I meant no harm. It did cause the pull to lessen. It was less aggressive and more curious. I suppose she had decided to watch me until she could figure out if I was friend or foe. I certainly didn't want to be the latter.

"So who are we having tea with?"

"Hatter, naturally." Dorian helped me over a fallen limb so that my gown did not catch on the branches. If I had known we would be traipsing through the forest, I would have chosen to wear breeches instead of a gown.

"Naturally," I replied back, my lips twisting down.

Dorian laughed at my expression and he drew me to him, rubbing his nose against mine. "Do not look so worried, my peach. Hatter is a good friend of mine, you have nothing to fear."

"But your mother said I had everything to fear here," I countered.

My prince's lips turned down in a frown. "That may be true but only in certain company. But since you are with me, you should be well enough." He kissed my knuckles, and we were off again.

Somehow his words did not reassure me, and as we moved further into the forest, my wary feeling got worse. The pulsating sounds I had heard before had dissipated and in its place was laughter. High pitched maniacal laughter.

"What is that?" My footsteps slowed the closer we got to the boisterous sound.

"It is just a bunch of Fae having a good time." He shot me a wicked grin before he upped our pace until we were almost running.

My breathing increased as I tried to keep up with his long strides. I had lived my life caged. My body wasn't ready for such excitement, no matter how much my heart yearned for it.

I kept up with Dorian as best as I could. Embarrassingly, he had to pick me up when I tripped over my own two feet until eventually he finally stopped.

"Are you ready for this?" Dorian asked, his hand poised and ready to push back the brush that separated us from a noisy gathering on the other side.

As the laughter increased to a frightening level, I wasn't so certain I wanted to know what was on the other side. That was until I heard a familiar voice. One of a Ms. Liddell.

What was she doing here?

CHAPTER 14

DORIAN

I WATCHED LYNNE'S FACE as we stepped out of the dark forest and into the open area that housed Hatter's home. I wanted to give her something exciting but also make her aware of the differences between our worlds.

The Seelie Court was full of structure and rules, but the UnSeelie Court did not have those kinds of restrictions. Passion and fun were on the minds of almost every Fae in the kingdom, and no one knew about those more than Hatter.

When Lynne took in the scene before us her eyes widened and her mouth dropped open slightly. It was adorable, and it caused my body to tighten inappropriately. I had had my betrothed more times than I could count the last few days. One would think I would be tired of her. Alas, the more I had her the more I craved her touch and her wit. I couldn't wait to see how she reacted to Hatter and his friends.

"Come." I took her by the hand and led her into the clearing. A long table covered with a red tablecloth sat in the middle and surrounded by mismatched chairs that suited its guests perfectly.

"Hello, Hatter," I greeted the fae sitting at the head of the table. The silver-haired fae stood from his seat at my voice and welcomed me with a smile.

"Your highness, how good to see you!" his long silver hair cascaded around him as he moved from the table to my side. He held a hand out to me, which I clasped with my own. Then his gray eyes landed on my betrothed. "Now, who is this beautiful creature? This could not be the one that is betrothed to our dark prince. She is too magnanimous."

Lynne laughed at Hatter's obvious flirtations, which I brushed off. Hatter may flirt but he was harmless. He knew where he stood and what I would do should he touch what was mine. And Lynne was most definitely mine.

Even though I trusted my friend, I wrapped an arm around Lynne's waist and hugged her to my side. Giving her a small smile, I said, "My peach, this is Hatter and these," I gestured to the creatures sitting around the table, "are his permanent guests."

"More like infestations," Hatter muttered but grinned, nonetheless.

"How rude." A three-foot mouse with a wood door latched to his chest sniffed. "I'm not some rodent."

"Could have fooled me!" a black creature with large wings and a twinkle in his eyes cackled.

"Oh, knock it off. Can't you see we have royalty present?" an opalaught with ragged ears and beady eyes snapped.

Ignoring the arguing of his friends, Hatter returned to his seat. "Please, please have a seat we were just sitting down to tea."

"You are always having tea." I led Lynne over to the table and pulled out a chair for her. I took the seat next to her on Hatter's right hand and proceeded to pour my betrothed some tea.

"Too true." Hatter nodded picking up his own tea. "But with my new lovely guest, it's hard to not want to celebrate all the time."

At first, I thought he was talking about Lynne, but Hatter's eyes went right by her and to the blonde human I had not noticed sitting at the other end of the table.

"Ms. Liddell, I did not know you were back again." I took a sip of my tea, my eyes watching her carefully. The girl had come to the UnSeelie Court more and more as of late, and I worried we might have a problem. Humans that became obsessed with us usually died tragically, and I didn't want that to happen with Lynne nearby.

"I hadn't left." Ms. Liddell took a sip of her tea, her eyes hazy from the effects. Hatter's concoction was almost as strong as faerie wine, which meant to us Fae we got little more than a slight high but to humans, the effects were tenfold.

"How much tea have you been giving her, Hatter?" I asked suspicion in my voice.

"Not much at all really." Hatter shrugged. "I make sure to give her a weak batch if that helps your conscious."

"Not really." I shook my head. "You really should not be giving her any at all."

"Why?" Lynne spoke up from my side. "What harm could it do?"

I placed my hand on top of hers and smiled. "Remember how I said there were dangerous things on this side of the Fae world?" I waited until she nodded her head before continuing, "Well, Hatter's tea is one of them. Made of the mortuvious mushroom it's potent enough to send a Fae screaming through the dark forest and it's even worse for humans." I glanced sharply at Hatter. "It's not something you drink lightly."

"Then why are we drinking it now?" Lynne stared down into her glass with a deep frown creasing her face.

"Don't you have any sense of adventure?" Ms. Liddell asked in a condescending tone. I shot her a warning glare, which only caused her to smile.

"I have a perfectly fine sense of adventure," Lynne growled, "I just don't fancy being drugged my first trip out of the palace."

This made Ms. Liddell laugh. "My God, let the girl out of your bedroom for more than a few minutes. Thank goodness, you didn't hover around me that much when I first came. I mean, that one time I had decided to skinny dip in the pond by the brownies villa was quite fun, don't you think?"

Hatter cackled along with her, but my eyes were on Lynne. She had begun to frown harder. I could see the wheels turning in her head as she tried to process what Ms. Liddell had said. No doubt Lynne thought something was going on between us, which was what Ms. Liddell had probably meant to happen.

"That is not how it happened and you know it, Ms. Liddell," I snapped, but the damage was already done.

"I think I'm about ready to go back now." Lynne sat her cup down and pushed her seat back. She nodded to Hatter. "Thank you for having me, it's been...informative."

She ran from the table before I could catch her, and I hurried to go after her. The dark forest was no place for the likes of her to be venturing into alone. Especially not after she had drunk some of Hatter's concoction. I was now wishing I had never brought her here in the first place.

I RUSHED AWAY FROM the tea party and into the dark of the forest. Before the forest had made me nervous but now with anger and jealousy in my heart, it only fit my mood.

The nerve of her. Who did she think she was? She was nothing but a puny little human. She should be worshiping at our feet not insulting us.

"Peach!" Dorian's voice called out to me, but I didn't slow down.

"Is it true?" I growled when he finally caught up to me. My fists clenched at my sides and I fought back the anger that had manifested itself in me so easily.

"Is what true?" he asked reaching for me but I jerked away. I didn't want him to touch me right now. If he touched me, I might very well fall apart. Even now I could feel my magic sizzling along the surface of my skin looking for an outlet.

My eyes darted down to the earth. It would be so easy to place my hands on the soil and change this dank forest into my own.

Shaking the temptation off, I glared at Dorian. "That you went skinny dipping with that human. Is it true?"

"What?" his eyes widened. "Of course not! Well, actually," he paused and rubbed the back of his head with a skittish grin, "it did not exactly happen like that."

"Then how did it happen?" I crossed my arms over my chest.

Dorian sighed and stepped closer to me but didn't try to touch me. "Look, you have to understand, Ms. Liddell is an immature brat that does not know how to keep her nose out of things. Which means she needs to be rescued a lot."

"What does skinny dipping have to do with you rescuing her? Was her clothing attacking her?"

He laughed slightly. "Actually, it was. She had gotten into a patch of brusselbutch, and if you had ever been in contact with that particular bush you would know that it burns like the Reaper when it touches your skin. So, I had to pull her out of the bush and in the process ended up getting myself covered in it. Thus causing us to have to take all of our clothing off."

I chewed on my bottom lip at his explanation. I'd never heard of a brusselbutch and wouldn't know the first thing about if it burned the skin or not but his story made sense. I tried to still the jealousy in me, but it was hard. I'd spent my whole life pretending not to feel things and now that I had the freedom to feel what I liked when I liked it was hard to go back the other way.

"Lynne," he whispered, his hands wrapped around my upper arms. This time I didn't pull away from him. I let him draw me closer. "Nothing has or ever will happen between me and that human. You are the only one for me." He tipped my chin up with his fingers. "My peach, I love you. No one else."

He brushed his lips against mine and I softened. Throwing my arms around his neck, I let myself get lost in his kiss. Like he said, she was a brat. I should pity her not feel jealous of her.

After a moment, Dorian drew back from the kiss and smiled. "Now, let me show you this beautiful fountain that sits at the heart of the UnSeelie Court. It is so scandalous even your mother would laugh."

"All right." I giggled. "Show me this fountain of yours and then take me home and make love to me."

My words caused Dorian to stop laughing and his eyes darkened. "Actually, on second thought, the fountain is not that great. Let us retire home."

I smacked his arm with a grin. "No you don't, you promised me a laugh. Now you must pay up."

"Very well," he sighed in defeat and then smirked, "But then we will spend the rest of the evening in my bed."

"Oh, the horror." I mock fainted as Dorian clasped my hand in his and led me out of the dark forest.

The UnSeelie Court was ever changing. One second you are standing in a dense forest and the next you are stepping out of the trees and onto a cobblestone road.

"Come, it is this way." Dorian held onto my hand tightly as he took me through a stone archway and into what looked like a maze.

"You UnSeelie are really into defense, aren't you?" I commented as we moved through the maze. Each twist and turn looked the same as the last.

"Like I said, the best offense is a good defense, and we do not lack for defenses." He paused for a moment and turned to me with a serious expression. "You have to promise me you will not wander on your own. At least not until after we have married. I do not want you to accidentally get swallowed by something."

I gulped. Swallowed? That didn't sound good.

"I promise."

"Good." He nodded and then started walking again. This time he didn't stop until we heard the sound of water. "We are almost there." He tossed me a grin before picking up his pace, almost running down the path.

I laughed and held my skirts to keep up with him until we came to the end of the path. The path exited into a square area surrounded by stone walls. Each corner had a tree in it and then in the center sat a fountain. As we approached the fountain, I began to understand why Dorian had said even my mother would have laughed at it.

The stone fountain had four women in a circle. They were scantily clad and their expressions were that of mid-orgasm. The designer had to be a man. There was no other explanation for it. As my eyes scanned up and down the figures I thought, a very sexually deprived male.

"How can you allow this to be in your kingdom?" I asked, not really upset but more curious. My mother would never have allowed such a thing. Sure the Seelie Fae were all for showing off their bodies at parties but outside of that, it was all about decorum.

"Believe me, we have tried to get rid of it, but every time we destroy it it shows back up in a few days." He placed a booted foot on the edge of the fountain. "Either it's the UnSeelie Court messing with us or there are some really fast satyrs around here."

"Satyrs?"

"Yes, half goat, they are pretty into the whole sex scene. Which is why you should never come here by yourself." He turned from the fountain and then froze. "Or one of those will show up." His eyes focused on something behind me.

Standing at seven feet tall was the biggest hairiest creature I had ever seen. He had large horns on his head and his legs were as thick as my whole body. His dark eyes briefly looked at Dorian but bypassed him and focused on me. The curl of his lips made my stomach drop.

Oh no.

CHAPTER 16

DORIAN

SATYRS, WHILE LARGE AND strong, were not the smartest of creatures and were purely focused on mating day in and day out. Any female had to keep their guard up and their legs firmly closed.

"Pretty lady," the satyr's deep voice said as his large steps caused the ground to shake around us. As he approached, his hand reached between his legs to grab himself.

Narrowing my eyes, I stepped in front of Lynne. "Stop where you are."

The satyr didn't even pay me much mind. One would think that he would recognize his prince and bow immediately at my feet, but the UnSeelie Court was not so organized. I was lucky if half the residents knew who I was, and since I spent the majority of adult life in as many female beds as I could find, I could only blame myself.

"Did you hear me?" I snarled. The satyr paused for a moment before his hand whipped out and slammed into me. My body flew away from Lynne and to the other side of the courtyard.

My head hit the ground hard, and I saw stars. Shaking my head, I scrambled to my feet as Lynne screamed. The satyr had cornered her by one of the trees and was reaching for her. Lynne's eyes were full of terror, and it made my insides burn.

I rushed across the courtyard and jumped onto the back of the large beast. Grabbing a hold of his horns, I growled, "Do not touch her."

"Get off, get off." The creature yelled shaking his head this way and that as he tried to dislodge me. I lost my grip on the fourth shake and fell to the ground with a thud.

Thankfully, I had angered the satyr enough that he moved away from Lynne and came after me. Not so lucky for me though because his hooves were sharp and slammed into my back before I could get away.

Searing pain shot through my back and I stifled a groan. The pain fueled my anger, and I struggled to my feet. If he wouldn't listen to reason than I had no choice but to use my magic on him.

Usually, I tried to keep my magical use to a minimum. It took a lot of energy and a lot of the times it caused more damage than I intended. This time though, it was either use it or get pulverized. If I was lucky, Lynne would get away unscathed even though I wouldn't.

I drew on the magic inside of me, making my skin come to life. I pulled it into my hands and prepared to attack the beast head on when it cried out in alarm.

My eyes jerked from my hands to the beast. Vines wrapped around its waist. They squeezed tightly causing the satyr to scream.

"Let me go!" he yelled fighting against the vines that only tightened more.

I let go of my magic letting it fall silent and then slowly moved around the large body of the satyr. What was on the other side made my brows rise.

Lynne stood by the tree with her hands on the trunk. Green strings of energy pulsated out of her and into the ground beneath her. More vines shot out of the ground and encased the screaming beast.

As I approached her, I noticed her eyes began to gleam with a bit too much enjoyment. The more the creature screamed, the tighter she coiled her vines around it. She didn't even notice me until I was right in front of her face.

"My peach," I said beside her and then when she didn't answer, I touched her shoulder and shook it, "Lynne, stop. You'll kill him."

"Good," she snapped, "the creature deserves it."

I frowned at her answer. "No. He does not. Satyrs are like this by nature. They can no more resist the need to mate than we can force ourselves not to need to breathe."

My words only made her lips curl down into a frown. "Then there is no use for them in this world. We should just get rid of them all."

"You cannot," I insisted my grip on her shoulder tightening, "we need the satyrs."

"Why?" she snapped.

"If war comes who will be on the front lines if not for them? They might try to take what they like but we still need them to fight our battles for us."

"That doesn't make any sense at all." She shook her head at me. "If they harm others, they should be put to death or banished. No good can come from them existing. My mother would never have let them live."

"But this is not the Seelie Court." I snapped. "We are UnSeelie, and we do not abide by the rules of your mother. Now, let him go."

She shot me a look, and for a moment I thought she might kill him anyways, but then the vines loosened and sagged releasing the satyr. The beast fell to the ground his breathing ragged.

"Come." I took hold of her elbow and led her away from the satyr and out of the courtyard.

We walked for a little while in silence until she finally spoke, "If I am to rule with you, we have to be able to agree when it comes to those situations. If I had had it my way, I'd have killed him without a thought. Nothing that vicious should be allowed to live."

I sighed. "That is the problem. You only see him as a vicious beast, but he is much more than that. Satyrs create music and even help build homes for our citizens. They cannot help that during mating time they cannot hold back their urges. It is just in their nature."

"Well, their nature is wrong."

I stopped and pulled Lynne into my arms. "That is not for us to decide," I growled and held her tight, "I was trying to make you laugh and here I made you angry."

Lynne's tense shoulders softened. "It's not your fault. I should have listened to you when you tried to tell me that things are more dangerous here than at home. I guess I still have a lot to learn about your world."

"And I'm sure there is even more to know about yours." I cupped her face in my hands and pressed my lips to hers. "Come, let us retire. I have some wounds that need attending to, and I know just the nurse to help me with them."

Lynne giggled as I winked at her before dragging her back toward the palace and away from the nastiness of the UnSeelie world.

CHAPTER

LYNNE

TOMORROW WAS MY WEDDING day. I would finally be with Dorian forever and never have to be caged again.

Normally, one would not see the groom the day before the wedding, bad luck and all that, but I couldn't help myself. I wanted to see him. I needed to see him.

When I rose for the day, I quickly dressed and skipped down the stairs of the UnSeelie Palace. The wedding would be held on this side of the Fae Realm as was tradition. My mother would arrive tomorrow for the big day but not a day sooner. Typical.

Others had already begun to arrive though. The palace was busy with life.

Servants ran to and fro, each in a hurry to get everything ready for the biggest royal wedding of the millennia. Fae lived for a long time, so it was safe to say the leadership didn't change often. Royal weddings were a rare event indeed.

Everything had to be perfect.

I hurried through the halls trying my best not to get run over by the UnSeelie Fae that filled the halls. Dorian usually was in his study at this time of day. He wasn't one to sleep in. He said he always worked best as the sun rose.

My lips curled up, a memory of the night before filled my head. Dorian had lavished me with his attentions not only once but several times until we both collapsed, and still, he'd woken with the morning light. At least I wouldn't have to worry about my prince being lax in his royal duties. Or his husbandly duties.

I rounded the corner that led to his study and paused at the door. It was closed as usual. I knocked on the wood but didn't wait for him to answer before turning the knob.

Peeking my head in, I frowned. He wasn't here. I pushed the door completely open and stepped into the room.

A large desk took up most of the room. The walls were lined with bookshelves stuffed with so many books I'd had to stop myself from drooling the first time I saw them. When we weren't getting lost in each other's bodies, I loved to sit and read by his side while he worked. But today I wouldn't get either of those because my prince wasn't to be found.

Not to be deterred, I left his office and searched out his mother, my soon to be mother-in-law.

I had noticed that when the UnSeelie Queen wasn't in her garden, she spent an awful lot of time in her bedroom. I'd come across her bedroom door ajar once. She had been standing in front of a large full-length mirror that took up most of one of her bedroom walls. It had been quite peculiar; she had just been staring at it. The longing in her eyes made me want to ask, but since I wasn't her blood, I thought it best to keep my mouth shut.

But still, it was curious. What was she looking at?

Shaking my head clear of the thought, I knocked on her bedroom door. Her voice called out from the other side and I opened the door.

Sure enough, there she was standing before the mirror once more. For a moment, I thought I saw something in her reflection but the moment she saw me it was gone.

"Good morning," I said walking toward her. "I don't mean to barge in unannounced, but I was wondering if you had seen your son today?"

"You know it's bad luck to see the groom before the wedding," she chastised, but her lips curled up in a knowing grin.

"I know." I glanced down and shuffled my feet. "But I just have this feeling like I have to see him."

"Very well." She moved across the room, her skirts brushing the hard floor with a swishing sound. "He mentioned something about going to his spot this morning."

My eyes lit up at her words. If he was at the tree, we could be alone without interruption. Hopefully, we could get a few more embraces in before the others began to search for us.

"Thank you." I nodded and headed for the door, but her voice called out to me making me stop.

"While I do not abide by many rules, I feel as if you should follow today's. You should not see your prince today." There was a weird tone in her voice that I did not understand as if she knew something bad was going to happen.

"I will take it under advisement." I nodded again before leaving her room.

I really should follow her advice. It was said the UnSeelie Queen had the gift of foresight. Not like the Seer that knew all of the future, but enough of the gift that the feelings she got were pretty profound.

But I really wanted to see Dorian. Bad luck or not, I would take my chances.

The moment I stepped out of the hedge maze and into the orchard rain began to pour. That's odd, I thought frowning up at the sky. The rainy season had all but ended, which meant it was the best time for a wedding. But the liquid splashing against my face was undoubtedly rain. A sinking feeling settled in my stomach.

The UnSeelie Court had warmed up to me after my time here, and I hadn't gotten lost once in the last few weeks. The rain coming down now felt like a warning. Like it didn't want me to keep going.

First Dorian wasn't in his normal place, then the queen told me not to go, and now the realm itself was warning me away. To a sane person that would be a clear enough sign that I should turn back and not risk whatever was waiting for me. But all the signs just made me need to know what was so bad that I shouldn't see my one true love?

With a determination I didn't know I had, I hurried through the orchard. My hair plastered to my face and my skirts became wet against my legs. I forced my feet to take one step after the other as I made my way up the hill and to our normal meeting place.

When I reached the top, my heart plummeted. Before my head could finish processing what I was seeing, my feet were turning back the way I had come. I shouldn't have come.

My feet pounded through the wet grass, hitting puddles of mud that soaked my dress further, but I didn't care. All I could focus on was what I had just seen.

Dorian had been at the top of the hill, looking as dashing as ever, but instead of brooding like he usually did when he came there alone; he had his arms wrapped around Ms. Liddell. His hands were in her blonde curls, and he held her close to him as he ravished her mouth. Just thinking about it made me sick to my stomach.

I didn't know where I was going but I knew I couldn't go back to the palace. They would all be there getting ready for the wedding tomorrow. I cried out as a sharp pain sliced through my heart. I couldn't breathe.

I'd made it to the other side of the orchard. I leaned against the large rock wall that went around the whole area and tried to catch my breath.

A voice called out to me over the sound of the rain falling. I glanced up to see Dorian running down the hill with Ms. Liddell close behind him.

Shaking my head, I pushed off the wall. I couldn't see him. It was too soon. Too fast. I needed somewhere to think.

Then as if reading my thoughts, a bundle of bushes next to me shook and then moved aside to reveal a hole. Not thinking twice about it, I hurried into the hole bypassing a worn out sign as I trudged further into the opening.

The further in I went the larger the hole became until I was able to walk standing upright. When I exited the hole, I was in a stone covered dome. Standing in the middle of the area was a single tree. It was large and glowing with brightly colored fruit, it was as if it had been waiting for me.

My feet kept going toward the tree, never stopping to wonder what they were doing. When I stopped before the tree I heard a voice in my head. It was deep and warm. The sound of it resonated through me pushing away the chill of the rain.

"What do you wish?" It asked.

Wish? My brow crinkled, not sure if it was some kind of trick or not.

"Your heart aches."

"Yes," I said aloud even though the words had been in my head.

"Do you want it to stop?"

I swallowed thickly and thought back to what I had just seen. Dorian had told me nothing was going on between him and the human woman, but he had lied. Even after all the signs had pointed to it I had believed him because I loved him. But clearly, he did not love me.

If I wished I could turn back time. Then I would never fall in love with the dark prince. I wouldn't know what it felt like to have my heart ripped from my chest.

Decision made, I stepped closer to the tree and answered, "Yes."

"Then take our fruit and you shall get your wish."

My eyes looked to the fruit above me. They were about the size of a peach but with a glow that came from deep inside. The thought of peaches made the fist around my heart clench once more.

Not being able to stand it any longer, I grabbed the nearest fruit from the tree and held it in my hand. Warm to the touch it tingled throughout my palm. I slowly brought it up to my mouth and then with my wish in mind, I took a bite.

The juices filled my mouth instantly and then my world was spinning. Everything I had ever known or felt rewound. It was like I was a spectator to my own life, except it was in reverse. I saw Dorian and Ms. Liddell embracing and then yesterday when I had been with Dorian myself. He looked at me with such love, and I wanted to stay in that moment forever, but the fruits magic pushed forward faster and faster until I couldn't make out the scenes in front of me.

Until finally, there was nothing.

CHAPTER 18

DORIAN

THE MORNING BEFORE MY wedding I had gone to my office like always to get some work done before the day began. When I arrived there was a note on my desk from Lynne asking me to meet her at our usual spot.

I almost didn't go. It was bad luck to see the bride before the wedding and Fae were anything if not superstitious. I wished I had listened to that warning in my head but being the lovesick fool I was I hurried out of my office and headed to the orchard.

At just after dawn, the orchard was quiet, no workers or anyone else in sight. I thought nothing of it and made the usual trek up the hill to my tree. When I arrived I was happy to find Lynne already waiting for me.

She was dressed in a pale blue dress that clung to her curves. She took my breath away. I couldn't get enough of her. Soon she'd be my bride and then we wouldn't have to worry about sneaking around to be together.

"Hello, my prince." She smiled at me from beneath her lashes. She had a shyness to her that was unusual for our relationship. I'd had her every way I could have her, how could she still be shy around me?

Shaking off her strange behavior, I took her in my arms. "Hello, my peach," I purred sliding my hands down her back and cupping her backside.

She made a small squeaking noise but didn't pull away. I gave her a confused look. "What's wrong? You act like I've never touched you before."

"Nothing, nothing. Just wasn't expecting such a warm welcome is all." She gave me a shaky smile that made me frown harder.

"Well, we are getting married tomorrow, I would hope that all of my welcomes are like this." I stroked my thumb across her face searching for the difference that I just couldn't put my finger on.

"I'm sure they will be." Lynne ducked her head down, a blush coloring her cheeks.

"You are not having doubts now, are you?" I pulled back slightly, concern on my face. I thought we were doing great. Wonderful even. "If there is something I have done please tell me and I will remedy it right now."

"No, no." She shook her head and then chewed her bottom lip like I had seen her do a million times. The nervous habit was so familiar that it calmed some of my fears.

"Then what is it?"

She gave me a soft smile. "I just wanted to see you is all. I missed you."

Rain began to fall between the leaves of the tree sprinkling us with water. I frowned up at the sky. It shouldn't be raining today.

Pushing away the thought, I turned my attention back to Lynne and cupped her face with my hand. "I have missed you as well." Intent on stilling whatever it was that was bothering her, I swooped down and claimed her lips with my own.

Right away I knew something was off. The lips I kissed were Lynne's. They felt like Lynne's and even the body was Lynne's, but the taste. It was all off.

A gasp from behind me had me ripping my mouth away from Lynne's. The sight before me made my heart stop and my blood run cold.

The unmistakable form of Lynne ran from me and down the hill. I turned from the other Lynne to the one standing before me determined to find out what was going on. But I didn't need to ask because it wasn't Lynne before me at all. Alice Liddell stood in Lynne's place, a nervous grin on her face.

"What have you done?" I hissed grabbing her shoulders.

"Just a bit of fun is all." She shrugged and tried to laugh it off.

How she had been able to transform into Lynne well enough to fool even me was a mystery. One that I didn't have time to solve, but I would as soon as I found my, no doubt, heartbroken princess.

"I will deal with you later," I snarled before running down the hill and after where Lynne had gone.

The rain was coming down harder now. As if the UnSeelie Court knew what was happening. Reaper forgive me for not listening to my gut when I got the message this morning.

I raced through the orchard and called out Lynne's name when her form appeared in the distance. My voice only seemed to make her flee because the next thing I knew she was gone. Not from running the other way but she disappeared altogether.

When I finally got to where she had disappeared I searched everywhere. But there was no sign of where she could have gone. Until the rain suddenly stopped.

The ground shook beneath my feet, and I had to lean against the stone wall of the orchard to keep my balance. A sick feeling filled me and I knew where she had gone.

Not bothering to let the bush let me through, I called upon my magic until it was a physical blue ball of light crackling in my hands. Blasting the ball at the bushes, I darted through them the moment there was an opening.

As I went through the hole that I had created, the bushes automatically began to grow back behind me. I shoved through the hole trying to get through before they caught up to me. The place I was going was a forbidden place. A place meant for only the direst of times. For it to let my princess through now of all times was something else entirely.

Were the gods playing with us? Could this be part of their plan? If so, I wanted no part in it. I just wanted my princess back.

I finally forced my way out of the hole and into the sanctuary of what we called the Tree of Life. The heart of the Underground, it was kept hidden from all that may try to take its fruit.

As I came into the clearing, I saw two different fruits on the ground before the tree. Both with a single bite in it. One was near the entrance and the other was next to the roots of the tree where one of them had come up like an arch to shield a form beneath it.

"Lynne!" I raced toward her body but before I could get to her, the ground took her into itself and the root of the tree settled on top of her.

"Give her back!" I screamed at the tree. I pulled my magic into my hands and blasted the tree but it didn't even move an inch. Since the tree wasn't going to budge for me, I focused my powers on the ground beneath the root trying with all my might to get the ground to give her back.

I poured magic into the earth until there was nothing left. The blockade in my energy kept me from going any further and using my own life force. I screamed in agony as the last of my magic faded away.

Yelling and cursing at the tree, I attacked it with my fists. I didn't care that it was sacred. I didn't care that I could kill everyone in the Underground. All that mattered was getting Lynne back.

"Your highness?"

The small bell-like voice called out to me ceasing my attack. Turning my back on the tree, my eyes landed on Alice. I stalked toward her, not even bothered that my hands were bleeding. It was time to get to the bottom of this.

DORIAN

ALICE LIDDELL SAT BEFORE me, tears glistening in her eyes but they did not move me. "I was only trying to help. The shadows said I could be one of you and I am. Look." She tried to extend a hand out to me, but I was too blinded by my rage to give her a second glance.

The area was dim and surrounded by a stone wall, closed off to everything else except a door-shaped hole where two guards stood awaiting my command. No one came here anymore. The tree before me was sacred, and it was forbidden for anyone to touch its fruit. Not just one person but two had tasted the sweet juices from the tree.

One being the human now turned Fae before me, and the other...my eyes trailed over to the tree. My peach. How could you? Sadness filled me for a moment before my rage returned.

"I'm quite aware of your new found abilities, Alice," I cursed causing the young girl to cringe, "did you think for a moment that the shadows could have lied? That they would tell you anything you wanted to hear? Just so you would do what they wanted?"

"But why would the shadows want to keep you apart? Surely they couldn't care less about your marriage?" She stuttered as she tried to rationalize her actions.

"You couldn't be more wrong." My laugh was bitter and heavy. "They have as much invested in my marriage as I do, except I had more to lose."

And I lost it all. My heart clenched like a troll had its hand wrapped around it and was tightly squeezing it with each breath. How could I have been so foolish? I should have realized what was happening. How was I so weak not to know the difference between real and fantasy?

"Why? What do they gain from breaking you two up?" Alice cocked her head like a child trying to understand grown-up things.

"That's the question, isn't it?" I hissed. I knew very well what the shadows wanted from us.

The Seelie Queen thought she was fooling everyone, but I knew what she had done. At least part of it. My mother did not keep many secrets from me and this was one that was too important to keep.

The Faes cast out by the Seelie Queen were not happy with their sentence. They wanted to come back. To be as they once were. But they had stayed in the Shadow Realm too long. There was no going back.

I knew that my marriage to Lynne was supposed to help us fight against them when they time arose but had I known the shadows were so close I would have been more careful. Made Lynne more aware of the danger.

But it was too late now.

"And you will have plenty of time to think about the answer. Guards!" My voice rose as my anger spiked. "Everything that happens from here on out is on your shoulders."

My words caused Alice to crumble into a heap of blue on the ground. Her cries racked her body and only grew louder when the guards wrapped their hands around her arms and dragged her away. I watched as they took her out of the area and then turned my back on her.

There was nothing left for me now. The one person I had ever truly loved was gone and the ones who had caused it was still out there. I couldn't let myself become weak again. The Underground couldn't afford for me to.

As I walked back to the palace, I came across the white roses I had been waiting to show Lynne. They had finally bloomed, and it was the perfect time to show them to her. Except she wasn't here to show.

I marched over to them intent on destroying the beautiful flowers when I saw that they weren't white at all. The edges of the petals had begun to turn red as if painted. The longer I stared at them, the more the white changed until eventually, all that was left were red roses.

The color made bile rise in my throat. Blood. They were they color of blood. Like the blood that was now on my hands. The hands that would have to tell the Seelie Queen what had happened. I could only hope that the next blood that would be spilled was my own.

MY FACE BURNED. I'D imagine that this was what it felt like to have hot pokers shoved into my face. Not that there was any physical injury.

There was no blood. Not cuts. But the swirling glyphs that now marred the left side of my face were foreign to me. As was the conversation being had while I lay on the hard marble floor of the Seelie palace.

"What are we going to do now?" the Seelie Queen hissed at my mother.

"Do not ask me. I was against this from the beginning," my mother snapped back.

"Well, it is your son's fault that all of our planning has been ruined in one day." The high-pitched screech that had become the Seelie Queen's voice caused me to wince.

I didn't know what they were discussing. I honestly didn't care. My heart ached almost as much as my face, and I could feel something nagging in the back of my mind trying to force its way to the forefront.

"And the human child is not to blame? You did not have to curse him. I would have made sure he was amply punished." My mother's eyes glanced to me with sadness. Why was she sad? This was my fault. I did this. I should be punished. If it weren't for me my peach, my love, wouldn't be gone.

"She's human no longer, my cousin. A poor imitation but Fae, nonetheless. No doubt the reward for her deceit." The Seelie Queen sniffed and crossed her arms over her chest. "I have punished her as well."

"Taking her head is far less of a punishment than what you have done to my son!" my mother's voice finally rose to echo off the walls of the throne room. "She may suffer, but he will suffer more and not even be able to do anything about it. Hardly fair for a royal Fae."

"I cannot show leniency. Especially now," the Seelie Queen tried to soothe my mother, "I understand how you feel. You are losing your son but at least he is not dead." The weight she put on the word permeated the room.

"Yes, I suppose not." This time my mother's voice was small and almost fragile. Usually, I would want to go to her. My own heart aching to comfort her in her sadness, but for some reason, I couldn't feel my usual empathy. In fact, my heart did not ache at all.

My eyes darted to the mirror the Seelie Queen had set up so I could see her work. The dark blue of my eyes had faded to a pale blue. The same exact shade as Lynne's. A sharp pang sent pain throughout my body, and the symbols on my face flared to life in a glare of light so bright I was blinded briefly.

"What have you done?" I could hear my mother screaming out beside me. Her hand touched my shoulder rolling me over to face her. Tears rolled down her face but instead of wanting to comfort her my lips curled up in a smile.

"As I said before, he will suffer for his grievances against the Seelie Court until we can find a replacement." The Seelie Queen smirked, clearly happy with her choice of punishment.

"But what does that mean?" my mother asked for me. I wished to know as well but the bubbling laughter filling my chest kept me from asking.

"Your dear prince will not be able to mourn his lost love. It's a blessing, really. He should thank me." The cruel smile on her face did nothing to stop the laughter from falling out of me.

I jerked away from my mother's hand and clutched my stomach. I tried to force the laughter back, to remember that I should be upset, but the more I tried to reign in the feeling the more my face burned.

"You are an evil witch," my mother's voice snarled as she stared down at me in disbelief.

"We all do what we have to for those we love," was the Seelie Queen's response.

She turned from my mother and snapped her fingers at a guard. "You, call for the Cheshire and Poppy. It is their turn to serve their kingdoms."

"Of course, your highness."

The laughter finally dissipated, and I lay on the cold floor catching my breath. The words of the arguing royals faded away and while my face still burned from the spell, I could feel something new in my heart. An inkling that had not been there before.

This was only the beginning.

THANK YOU FOR READING!

Want to find out what happens to Kat next?
Find out in Chasing Rabbits.

Don't stop there! Find out how it all started with Alice's story.
Alice's story: The Crimes of Alice

Don't want to interact but want to be on the up and up?
Follow me on Social Media
Facebook.com/erinrbedford
@erin_bedford

Join my new release newsletter.
Erinbedford.com/newsletter